Student in the Underworld

Irving Warner

Livingston Press
University of West Alabama

Copyright © 2020 Irving Warner
All rights reserved, including electronic text
ISBN 13: trade paper 978-1-60489-267-3
ISBN 13: e-book 978-1-60489-269-7

Library of Congress Control Number 2020940001

Typesetting and page layout: Taylor Donato
Proofreading: Tricia Taylor, Joe Taylor, Erin Watt,
Angela Brooke Barger, Nic Nolin

Cover Design: Taylor Donato

Student in the Underworld

"We think we are straight in our justice,
No anger from us against those
Who hold out pure hands."
The Eumenides, Aeschylus

1.

Student Patterson looked under his bunk for Ensign Fremont in their so-called 'stateroom.' It was the size of a large pizza oven with no shelves. Their space was the smallest human abode on the *U.S.S. Refrigerator Transport 125-A* named after no one, launched prematurely — before anyone thought to name it. Or cared to?

Fremont hid there — butt out, face towards the bulkhead buried in a pillow. If only Fremont's situation were simple such as *mal de mer* rather than rank cowardice.

"Fremont, the Captain said he would have you shot if you abandon your post again."

"My father is Secretary of the Navy. They wouldn't dare. I hate high seas. I'm scared, Student. All we're doing is packing prime rib and ice cream for the black market in Saigon. I'm in the Skull and Cross Bone Society. I was president of my class at Yale. I shouldn't be here."

Student stood, yanked the kink out of his back — braced himself as the next 50 footer swept under the "Bugly," short for Butt Ugly, the sly nickname the 40 man crew had for their ship. It is the spring of 1968, and soon all this sea faring nonsense will be over for him.

He went forward 25 feet to the bridge. The helmsmen and quartermaster's mate looked at him — both treating themselves to a smirk. They loved cowardice in officers.

A blue-green monstrosity parented by seawater and doom — one in a succession of six or seven thousand — swept the entire 350 foot length of the "Bugly." Southern seas poured into the gaping hole where the 2.5 inch deck canon stood before being ripped out.

"You think she'll sink with that hole in her, Lieutenant?"

"No. The watertight doors are double there."

"We're sure as hell heavy in the bow. We might founder. Where is Ensign Fremont, Lieutenant?"

They each mimed concerned glances — but if foundering were possible, the rat-bastards would be fighting each other over the only lifeboat not caved in or rotted out. Best to keep his officer-distance and not answer.

In fact, like anyone on the ship, the two carrion eating fowl knew where Fremont was. They knew where *everyone* was in rough seas. They were, with the exception of Lieutenant Anderson, at their post mostly drunk, stoned or both, or in their bunk hanging on.

Lieutenant Anderson, recently of Annapolis, Maryland, was the senior lieutenant on the "Bugly" the day Student reported for duty in San Francisco. Student had eleven months left of his three-year active duty. Anderson was full of navy acronyms:

"I'm the OD, you're the JOD and the little shit being carried across the dock in a wheelbarrow is the ExO, and the guy supervising the swabbies pushing the wheelbarrow is our God-Don't-You-Know-It captain."

Student's presence on the Bugly was a bumper-harvest coincidence of history and dumb chance.

He originally signed up in the Navy ROTC program in 1960 — years before Southeast Asia melted into America's tar baby. He had gotten two degrees out of the deal, and now he had nearly served all his years of active duty, 'Glory Be to His Wisdom,' as they said at his church in Iowa.

The concluding twelve months was sea duty. He had become bored with teaching English at an obscure base. To the horror of his fiancé and colleagues at the easy-does-it navy base in Michigan — he had volunteered for this experience.

He went from bored on land to bored at sea — on a freezer ship shuttling monotonously between San Francisco and the Mekong Delta, downriver from notorious Saigon.

This was the western-leg of his last trip. He did not want to be an OD, a JOD — or any other military acronym for the rest of his life. This was the much-planned point where he would spend the remainder of his days as quietly normal, contented and modestly provided as a Ph.D. in English might allow. He and Debbie would settle into a midwestern town's college community, raise their family and take in literary readings by wandering artists from far flung locales.

All would move towards completion when he reported directly to graduate school in San Francisco after sea duty. Debbie would join him there; they would joyfully wed after a three-year engagement. This was the halfway point to normalcy. At the completion of his Ph.D. Debbie looked forward to their permanent home with name-brand zeal.

> *"And our home will have Edgington Dutch doors, Stu. I just love Dutch Doors with the rich old wood tones."*

Debbie had been surveying diverse publications on house design since high school and Student accordingly admired her for it.

With a societal stamp-of-approval-on-the-buttocks in three years, they would move back possibly to their home state of Iowa, savor the good life with modesty and watchful moderation.

It just wasn't to be.

Seers of Future Present

(Elder Men and Women dressed in flowing robes and wearing sandals)

Oh Student, you wretched man, your hopes and dreams are all for nothing. Your future has turned into a featureless plain of desiccated cow flops. True, Debbie began her teaching credential at the University of Wisconsin when you began your year of sea duty. She also discovered sex and radical politics, all in a single package beginning with a chap named Sean. He saw her coming with corn growing out of her ears, and she was a Godsend for him, and as it developed, quite a few others.

And that is not all: Poor man, you are about to start one of the most catastrophically and colossally discombobulated graduate programs in the history of American collegiate education. If you ever get a Ph.D. it will be a miracle. We are the only chance you have, and frankly, we aren't optimistic.

2.

Student sat in the college cafeteria trying to find a comfortable position. He was given his active duty discharge paperwork at Fort Mason that morning along with his last mega-shot of antibiotic. Hopefully this would mow down the last desperate rush of Southeast Asia bacteria.

His first conference with the mysterious Dr. Jenkins, his major professor, was tomorrow morning. He had until morning to move out of the Bachelor's Officers Quarters.

Tomorrow morning was a big damned deal.

He still felt vaguely sick from the latest course of antibiotics. His crotch was still raw from the awful pink ointment he applied each morning, and the remnants of the boils on his legs still itched like mad.

"Congratulations, Lieutenant. You almost caught the full inventory of whorehouse uglies in Saigon: You have crabs, clap, and cankers. How did you overlook syphilis and head lice?"

The letter throwing him over from Debbie, his fiancée — the girl he had dated since Junior High — had devastated. The letter was waiting for him at Saigon Harbor. Her Dutch Doors had gone up in a surge of hostility towards the military and matters sexual.

"Stu, you really have to recognize you are a killer and atone, plus appreciate how throttled we were sexually. Sex, through the orgasm, is a wholesome part of our expression as individuals."

At Saigon, once again, he had been eligible for extended shore liberty. This time, he would take it. While waiting for the shuttle into Saigon he admitted to an ensign named Hobbs that his only sexual partner had been Debbie, and not by much. At age 28, he had almost zip for experience. Hobbs suggested a Saigon bordello located on a scenic canal catering only to officers,

"Don't be shy, Student. Tell them of your situation: Say, 'I want to bong-bong in every known position using every known method,' and Miss Lee will oblige. She's really a nice lady. Has great girls, not one of them over 15, with cute little suction-cup shaped mouths. You will graduate from there with an advanced degree in screwing, guaranteed."

Before he even reached Miss Lee's he heard news every sailor bent on whoopee dreamed of: An internecine grievance in a black market deal resulted in someone sabotaging the *Bugly* so it would need an extra week to unload.

Student's descent into the darkness was thereby extended to better partake in complete carnal saturation.

Two months later and 6,000 miles away in the city of Saint Frances, he looked down at an untouched, anemic cafeteria sandwich. He was 15 pounds lighter, blighted with drugs and ointments, and could not have alcohol or sex for thirty more days. But by Jove and other diverse deities, he did know how to screw.

"How can you face people having killed innocent children in Vietnam?"

Two very young men sat across from him; Student wore civvies, but at once supposed his haircut stood out as if he'd worn a hedgehog for a hat.

"What are you talking about?"

Their eyes shone with the light of youthful virtue.

"You were in the military, right?"

"No. Now I don't feel well, so go away before I huck on you."

And they did, for he was close to it.

'Pastor, I will never have sexual intercourse for the rest of my life.'

'Don't be silly, Lieutenant. You just must be more prudent. More significant was that you spent the entire eleven days intoxicated. Have you had problems with alcohol before, Student?'

'No.'

He had lied then to the Navy Chaplain, just to get the mandatory sessions with him over and done — part of the military punishment for contracting venereal disease. While checking off from the *Bugly* his captain looked up from his textbooks on investment, scanned Student's personnel file and immediately stared at the doctor's report.

"Well I'll be switched, Lieutenant; I thought you something of a prude. Since you're signing off today — tell me how you got the first name?"

"My parents are farmers and by naming me 'Student.' thought they would give me a push to get a lot of education, Sir."

The Captain thought about that while turning over the doctor's report several time and drawing a breath.

"Well, I can make this go away. Don't want folks years from now reading about your escapade in Saigon. Jesus, you were naked when the shore patrol picked you up?"

"Yes Sir."

He was about to ask about that and Student tensed; he didn't have an answer. But the Captain, very corrupt but a decent sort, shrugged. He stood, extended a hand — an uncaptain-like gesture of good will.

"Lieutenant, good luck, damn it all. It is a rough world out there and you're a good officer and I'm giving you a fine evaluation. You ever want to jump back onto active duty, you'll be welcome."

Reflecting back on the recent offer to return to active duty caused him to gag. He was about to sprint for the men's room when an older man carrying a briefcase sat down — taking the place of the righteous twins.

"You Student Patterson?"

"Yes."

"I'm Don Jenkins, your major professor. How in hell did you ever get the name of 'Student?'"

He told him. How Jenkins found him in the cafeteria was part of the Jenkins mystique.

"Looked at your transcript. You don't know crap about folk lore or theater. Not one goddamned unit. Thought your M.A. was in drama, at least."

"No. Thesis was causality in *Measure for Measure*."

"Hmmm, I don't think the interview committee knew what the hell was going on."

He rested his arms on a briefcase festooned with anti-war stickers; an edge of it was chewed on, as if used in warding off guard dogs.

"You know that my program — the grant — is a bridge between theater and the folklore of the early labor movement."

"No, I didn't. "

"Beautiful. Well, by tomorrow morning come up with a reason why I shouldn't either disqualify you, or tack on about 18 classroom units in theater and craft. The goddamned interview process was really fucked up. Assholes."

And he was gone.

Student dragged out the envelope from the graduate school and re-read his fellowship acceptance, reassuring himself his overall appointment was secure. The program? Well, what the hell did he care about labor movements or Labor Theater? He could always do a straight Ph.D. in anything. With the *summa cum laudaes* on his record, someone would pick him up.

"You Mr. Patterson — teaching section 35, English 101?"

He looked up at a scruffy woman in her thirties. Forties? He couldn't tell. She wore old jeans and a man's shirt, shirttail out, and he at once imagined her old man home watching television and drinking beer.

She looked down at him — brow furrowed. How in hell were people locating him? She saw the question,

"I asked at the English Department office and they described you. The haircut really stands out." She smiled, asking, "You just get out of the joint?"

He didn't like her — rarely liked older freshmen students; they presumed too much, like this one who was very long-in-the-tooth for a freshman. He ignored the lousy joke.

"I'm Mr. Patterson, yes." He took out another paper from his folder, and there it was, Section 35, MWF at 10:00 a.m. That was OK.

She held her punch card from registration — between thumb and index finger, nails pretty much absent; hands looked like she set pins or washed dishes.

"I need your approval to get in."

"Why?"

"I didn't take the placement test. I worked."

"Then take it."

"Then I would miss the first two classes."

"Come anyway, and then take it."

"I don't want to take the test. It is ten dollars."

"I'm new here. I don't want to start out by bending rules, Miss, ah . . ."

"I'm Jessica Bolton. You sure you can't?"

"I'm sure I should not. Sorry."

She left. No further word.

Well, he mused . . . *got rid of that pain-in-the-ass.*

The sandwich lurked on the table. Student tried to concentrate hard enough to make it slither away, jump to the floor and run off.

He was ill and had no place to live. He would have to call home in Iowa again and listen to his mother weep for him being unable to visit.

"It has been over a year since we've seen you, son."

Student loved her like a son would a kindly mother. But he could wait before going home — gain a bit of weight. Plus, they probably did not know about Debbie's change of stripes. Over the years she had become closer to them than her own parents, especially her father who was a bitter pill of humanity.

For the time being, Student had to regain a bit of orientation — also some motivation. Hell, gain just anything.

A young girl stood in the hall waiting for Dr. Jenkins when Student showed for his appointment. She wore a maxi dress strewn with diverse day glow lunar designs; flip flops peeked out from beneath the dress. Though a slip of a girl, she had enormous unbridled breasts with nipples the size of coat buttons.

She wept quietly and gracefully. Looking over at him with tragic huge blue eyes, she seemed extraordinarily innocent. He hoped her appointment didn't precede his. Student was selfish that way. Also just two hours ago when he checked out of the bachelor's Officers Quarters he decided to be angry at all women. He would be anti-woman, save for his mother and Aunt Lila. *Be that resolved.*

So in adherence to his new policy, Miss Whatever could cry herself slap-happy for all it mattered. She held her gaze on Student.

"I loved him, and he dumped all over me. Tell him I'm going to the Golden Gate Bridge and jump off."

She walked away, turned up the stairs, and the pathos of her request was just seeping through Student's dark mist when the voices rose in the stairwell: A high plaintiff tone, followed by one low and scornful — Jenkins.

"You're not jumping off a bridge. You are instead going to grow up, get your degree and learn the difference between sex and love."

Jenkins exited the stairs, came into view — straightened a few of his metaphorical feathers out and took hold of a wad of keys while striding to his office humming a tune. He was clearly in a better mood than yesterday.

"Come right in, Mr. Patterson. We'll get this business straightened out even if it takes us a half hour."

He glossed over Student's deficiencies in theater and folklore recommending he take a course in introductory theater, both lecture and practicum.

"After all, you will be directing actors in key dramas. Should know enough to tell them where to stand."

"Where?"

"The Haywood Theater at the Butcherstown Writer's Guild Hall. It is in downtown San Francisco, or thereabouts. A scummier neighborhood."

"Butcherstown Writer's Guild?"

"Their name — labor activist organization dating back to 1914—" suddenly he laughed — "fucking place reeks of dynamite." His laugh down-graded into a satisfied sneer. He leaned towards Student, lowering his voice "Dynamite — that's what we need now with the Johnson Administration, sons-of-bitches."

He returned his attention to his file. Then at once Jenkins' entire countenance locked into a mask like one who bit into a bad spot in an apple. He braced himself with courageous inhalation — his eyes remained locked on Student's file. Moving just arm and finger, he flipped a page and kept reading,

He looked up at Student — eyes moved up to his military style haircut — then back to the file. He did a brief nod, and wiped the pad of an index finger across his lower lip. Student guessed he had not known about his Navy service.

"Jesus Christ, you were an *officer* in the Navy?"

"Yes."

Jenkins leaned back in his chair; ancient springs cried out weakly. He shook his head as if to clear cobwebs after receiving a shot-to-the-chops in a sparring match. He muttered to the other Jenkins sitting somewhere invisible, "Well, I guess that explains the haircut. Why didn't you see that, Jenkins Old Boy?"

Student shifted — no need to respond. By God, he was only here a day, and the Old Boy was already talking to himself. Actually, Jenkins could not be much beyond 50. If that.

He picked up a pencil and tapped it against Student's file, drew a breath, and started afresh,

"Well, what is your attitude about the war? You were in it."

"I wasn't, actually, Dr. Jenkins. I served on a ship that transported frozen goods between the west coast and Vietnam."

"Same thing. The effort. Hell, it's 1968; didn't you realize there was a war going on?"

"Not when I signed up for the NROTC in 1960. It paid for my bachelor's and master's degrees. I owed them three years of active service after six years of college. My parents raise chickens and some corn. Always strapped for money."

Jenkins straightened — Student hoped he was remembering the Old American pro-Vietnam war spirit of rock-solid patriotic values. In it, people of poor or modest means worked themselves from poor circumstances to better. Not even the most far-seeing carnival Swami could have predicted the U.S. involvement in Vietnam in 1960.

Jenkins tossed the pencil onto the file, scratched his mane of long salt and pepper hair, only to find out he still wore his black Greek Fisherman's hat with the button reading, "Cops Kill."

He took off the hat.

"Well. As your major professor I strongly recommend you at once grow your hair out. If you have slow-growing hair, consider a goddamned wig for the interval period. And for Christ sakes when on campus teaching your classes, don't mention you were a goddamned officer in the Navy. For one, you'll never get laid."

"Yes. I can see."

He took out papers he needed to sign, scrawled upon them deftly, then raised a hand and pointed at him,

"Now, no hustling the freshmen girls! You hear the indignity I just had to endure — that little morsel in the hall?"

"Yes."

"That is the repair work I must do when my grad students work the aisles in their composition sections, the horny pricks. You're my only Ph.D. candidate. I jolly well expect better, understand?"

"Absolutely."

He slapped the top of his desk, reached down, struggled to open a bottom drawer with a broken handle, did so with a few curse words — took out a half consumed quart of *Wild Turkey*.

"OK. Old custom of mine. Drink to your success. Sorry, no cups."

Jenkins removed the top, took a prodigious hit, then handed it to Student — the one thing that he should not do with drugs coursing through his veins.

But, this was necessity.

He drank, if shyly.

Jenkins looked on, almost said something about the timid nature of his drink, but put the bottle away.

"Hot damn, but that is noble juice. So, here is a discount coupon from the *A Plus B Hotel* near the Btuchers Town Writer's Guild hall. You get 30 percent off — part of the grant."

Then he turned to other matters, which began when his phone bleated — a victim of too many slam-downs of the receiver. The interview over, Student heard Jenkins voice turn sour,

"No! No! We all get wet, or none of us, tell them that. The cops will put the fire hoses to us."

When Student left the building he noted the young girl had not jumped off the Golden Gate Bridge but sat on a bench. She looked at him passing, but he kept his eyes forward. The young thing was looking for a friend, any friend.

She wouldn't find one with Student, not with his new post-Debbie, post Dutch Door Credo. Not by a mile she wouldn't.

He paid for a week in advance at the Mark Hopkins Hotel, supposedly the best in San Francisco. Khrushchev had stayed there along with all of his Little Russians. This un-Iowan behavior was Student's massive post-military splurge — wheedling away at his horde of savings dating from age seventeen when he and Debbie first started making plans. *'You two are planners,'* her parents praised, foolishly equating parsimony to intelligence.

He took half of his savings in his post-Debbie aftermath and sent it to his parents, who were always close to nothing. He meant for them to use it, but they would of course not spend a dime.

But it was time to cease this reflective boogie woogie and get down to some real rock and roll. He called the representative of the *Butchers Town Writer's Guild* (BTWG) and without thinking suggested they meet for lunch at his hotel.

"You've got to be kidding."

The voice was pure disbelief, as if he'd invited them to a pot-luck at the City Morgue.

Student wheeled and turned, rhetorically speaking, "Where would you suggest? I'm new here, of course."

The dialogue was repeated to someone next to the speaker, and there was polite female laughter then, "Why don't we meet at the Guild Hall? That is where the Haywood Theater is."

They rang off and that ended Student's first contact with the Chairman of the Haywood Playhouse, the Thespian arm of the Butchertown Writer's Guild.

Student fell into an unexpected frump in his room. Maybe it was the drugs. In any event Jenkins' bottle of whiskey reminded him of strong drink, and he had no business whatsoever of even *dreaming* of strong drink. He was capable of polite, drawing room imbibing until he fell under times of stress or despondency. Then alcohol contributed decisively to situations where at minimum he would make a grand horse's ass out of himself. The freshest example was Saigon, but not a first.

"Stu, please don't drink. It doesn't benefit you."

He remembered Debbie's frequent admonishments. *Damn*, he admonished himself, he had resolved *not* to recall Debbie, reminding himself of his new policy of misogyny. Despite his resolve, the momentum of his reverie pushed memories sullied by his past failure into play. There had been the misfire at the Cedar Falls Elks Club where of course Debbie was his date: 'What difference does it make,' he told her, 'if I got up on the table and imitated Eisenhower'?

Everybody thought it was a pretty darned good rendition.

Cursing these lapses against such useless rumination, he went to the window and looked down on San Francisco's California Street cable car struggling downhill towards Market Street — a massive insect, its mating call a string-activated gong.

Then his mind back flipped to his room's courtesy bar where tiny bottles of spirits dwelled. There were a dozen of them, maybe more! A potpourri of things wonderful. But, there were still medical and pharmacological issues resulting from his last liquor-laden wing-ding,

"If you drink, it reverses the effects of the antibiotic, and you will just have to do it over again."

Since all sex was out, he couldn't even masturbate, one of the purest forms of proactive countermeasures to womankind. Student must rely on humanity's great literary works to save and advise: What finer use than his background in literature to help him vault over life's chasms.

He lay in the middle of the bed and concentrated on Hippolytus, Euripides' great misogynistic hero. Chaste, utterly intellectual, the endlessly cocky Hippolytus ended up batted around by powerful women — a shuttlecock in a game of myth and metaphor. In the end, the poor devil took it in the neck.

Student lay there thinking of the legendary Hippolytus — he had done his Bachelor's Thesis on him, and it was such a brilliant paper he used it with the board to have his NROTC grant extended through graduate school. One of them even knew to who or what Hippolytus referred.

He began to toy with the idea of featuring Hippolytus as the opening play at the playhouse — the Whatever Playhouse, with Whoever playing the lead role, and someone like Kim Novak as Phaedra.

But then, Jesus! Who would play Aphrodite? Who would

play Artemis? Hell, who would play anyone? It was a blessing that in musing about this nonsense, Student drifted off. His last moments before sleep took over were listening to the bell of the same cable car coming back up from Market Street.

Ding, ding, ding goes the trolley.

Seers of Future Present

(Elder Men and Women dressed in overalls and granny dresses respectively)

Student, you poor unthinking devil. Look outside your own milky aura of personal concerns and bourgeois needs. You have embarked upon a path offensive to ancient feminine powers, and you are cruising towards a major bruising. You must learn to protect yourself from the slings and arrows of base fortune.

You must atone! Atone for your misdeeds and feckless ways, including drop-kicking the guileless Debbie into a virtual whirlpool of accomplished Lotharios and predacious masses of diverse reptiles who assume human form.

Yes! Atone! Otherwise you'll be absolutely screwed. As Freud wrote, and we paraphrase: *"Mankind's ass is grass and his own greedy, ego-oriented ways are the mower."*

3.

With the use of a map and the address, Student began afoot in search of the world headquarters of the Butchertown Writer's Guild, and within it, the Haywood Playhouse. Because of his unseemly high living at the Mark, he thought it would help him catch the spirit of the workers theater and walk to it.

He zigzagged and gawked his way downhill to the iconic Market Street, crossed it, found Mission, and continued towards the bay. Using his hard-won military experience, he located the approximate location of the Guild Hall on the map using the coordinate system. Hell, they were dealing with a man who had only recently traversed thousands of miles of open ocean carrying thousands of tons of prime rib and rocky road ice-cream.

And still Student continued south, then east. The sidewalks north of Market had been reasonably arrayed with youths in bell bottoms, girls in long dresses or flowing trousers. All had grandly long hair knotted back, loose, braided — all styles.

These would ordinarily not be hard to look at — these carefree couples cake-walked through the mine field of the late teens and early twenties. But they were fools! Student's age of idealism was recently tossed whole under the boxcar.

Plus, what a contrast in background — between that of children and a mature person struggling with harsh reality. None had plead with Ensign Fremont to come out from under their bunk and fight in the tradition of John Paul Jones and Admiral Farragut. Furthermore, one couldn't fully comprehend government's cavalier attitude towards human life until witnessing its ability to waste time, money, and all else upon the grand Orb. If there were any romance remaining, Debbie delivered the *coup de grace*. Yes! Student was now a universal cynic.

The further south-of-Market Student trekked, the more rough-around-the edges the ambiance until it took a nosedive into a stagnant pond of despair and want.

It went — half block by half block — from a weird hybrid of Henry Miller and Nelson Algren right down to Oscar Rockwell, the wino poet.

"I want to tell you, young man, how proud we are that some of our youth are not cowards, slackers, and communists like these awful hippies."

Two elderly women stood before him — blocking the way. *Jesus, but my military sticks out all over*, he thought, but in time it would go away.

They looked up admiringly, and Student managed a "Thank you, ladies." One's face squeezed into a half-hitch of pride and affection, a short thing — she reached up.

"I want to give one of our returning heroes a big hug. Come here."

And she did — hugged him while the other patted him on the shoulder. Despite his current strengthening credo he tolerated their attentions. After all, they were old women. Sexuality and clear mental processes were laundered from them by the many washings of brute age.

He threaded between the crones, thanking them again with something of a noble aside, and continued to the southeast. He held his course like the true mariner he'd become.

Doubt crept in when his surroundings became grimmer; had he taken a wrong turn — was this the sort of neighborhood for a playhouse? He took out his map and checked the address — on this heading the Gothic supports of the Bay Bridge formed an otherworld lace-work many stories overhead — gigantic support girders almost above him. The noise level increased.

The airborne dirt and grit resulting from the daily passing of tens-of-thousands of cars and trucks left grime and assorted road dirt everywhere. Many of the businesses were long shuttered, their owners migrating anywhere else for better times, or joining the ranks of forlorn residents who opted to give up. Sidewalks and gutters were littered with wine bottles, papers, and remnants of cardboard boxes. Some of the closed shop entryways smelled of urine, a few were still occupied by pairs or singles of street denizens who kept a keen eye set for a passerby.

"Hey, gotta smoke, partner?"

Student admitted to being a non-smoker and moved along.

But, there were stouthearted businesses who survived: On a corner "Artie's Eatery" was open.

Student would take repast here, consult his chart and even ask directions.

Artie's featured a surprise step-down entrance that nearly sent Student on a header into the counter and cash register. He caught himself with straight-arms to an Orphan's Fund Charity box and the counter itself. The empty fund box tumbled behind the counter empty.

Artie, or his employee, sat behind a counter. Against the window were booths.

"Watch that first step, it is a fuckin' Lulu."

Student unruffled himself, saw there was one other customer. He adorned the end stool drinking coffee, a pilgrim from life.

Student slid up on a stool, and looked at the wall menu — a sparse offering.

"What'll you have there, Sarge?'

"Not sergeant, Artie. Has the *officer* look about him."

The customer did notice things! He offered this correction, not seeming to care whether it was heeded or not.

Artie corrected himself with a chuckle, "OK, then General. What'll you have? Today's special is the chicken fried steak a la Calgary, with gravy over the fries, dessert, and coffee."

Student passed on that and went for the hamburger, then asked while he was poured a cup,

"Do you know where the Butchertown Writer's Guild is?"

The cook was in the middle of taking out an unambitious slab of meat from the refrigerator and putting it on the grill, but stopped; he made a half-turn towards him. The other customer did something of a belly-laugh, shook his head, and took a hit of coffee.

"What in hell would a guy like you want with a bunch of fly-blown commies like those fucks?"

Student at once regretted his stop, assessing an obvious lack of support by the owner. But, he *had* stopped here

"I have a meeting there."

The meat was put back in the refrigerator and grill turned down.

"Then go have your meeting, General. I'll not feed anyone connected with those pieces-of-shit. I *believe* in my country. That's ten cents for the coffee."

Student had only bills, and if the bastard wanted to make change, hell — he'd give him a twenty after what he just pulled. He reached into his coat and there was neither a twenty nor a wallet.

The old bags had picked it.

He checked his pockets. Nothing. His sad story of no-money was obvious by the time his hand came out of his pocket.

"And no money? Figures. Now get the hell out of my place."

While Student exited the customer blew some smoke at a ceiling stained with a tobacco mosaic of uncountable customers and offered, "The 'All Star Café' is just a block down. Ask there, they'll know."

Student was through with café hopping for the day. Hopefully, he'd still have his clothes by the time he reached the Haywood Playhouse — the bastion of the common man.

Taking out his map, realigning things — checking street signs — he pointed himself in the right direction.

Now the descent into desolation was industrial: Out-of-business shops ceased, stepping aside for giants: Capacious wooden buildings — gone to seed, converted to another use, or just collapsed from their own internal forces.

They decomposed solemnly where they were, death without fanfare.

When he reached his address, the building where the Guild was located was one of the largest. Yellow fire brick, cured to a jaundice hue, broadcast intrepidness — explaining why a structure of this mass would take a century or more to dissolve. Several letters on a sign displayed across the top story had gotten loose, inverted themselves — or just fallen off. It now proclaimed,

"PEERLES B TTLING"

Below were letters and numbers in smaller metal script reading

"Since 1879"

Peerless Brewing and Steam Beer stood six very large, irregular stories high, with a massive water tower occupying the roof, and even from street level, one could see this wooden edifice drooped. It did not impress anyone as earthquake proof.

Atop it stood a legion of pigeons — a fine edifice for their home aerodrome.

Odd projections of pipes and such emerged from Peerless's interior, held by rusted metal brace work, then trailed downward, disappearing into what Student assumed was a cavernous inner sanctum.

Though there were few windows, they yawned massive,

taking up two floors apiece. They were boarded over, the final shutters over the dead behemoth's eyes. Across the boarded façade of one was a sign equal in size reading, *For Sale: Fong Brothers Sales. HO-56980.*

Student assumed that the sign's intended audience was witless millionaires and/or investors with mental problems. Who else would assume ownership of a desolate building like this? And the Fong Brothers knew it. Student seized upon an image of the Brothers Fong hunkered over their Depression era phone invoking ancient Oriental Gods to bring them a victim.

In the street running before the feeble building old cable-car tracks with a central cable slot began and ended — each end paved over a half century ago? Thirty years? This, then, gave the frontage street the novelty of the shortest defunct cable-car route on the North American Continent, about 20 yards.

Student sleep-walked to the west, his mind hog-wrestling with reality: This crumbling troll beneath the Bay Bridge could no more be home to a guild hall than it might the final resting place of an Egyptian Pharaoh.

He stopped at a light pole; it leaned slightly streetward, its lens hanging loose, the bulb long shattered. At the base of the pole sat a man with a bottle between his legs — and not wine, but a whiskey bottle, half consumed. The flabby muscles on his face indicated he had attained the Nirvana of being grandly shit-faced. But he still had functioning vision.

"How ya' doin', brother? Hav'ah drink."

He offered Student the bottle, and the former Lieutenant was so shattered from the day's events, he took it, gave a swipe to the top, and allowed a good hit, handing it back. To hell with medication and recuperation.

"Thank you."

"My pleasure, brother. Name's Davy Boy."

"Glad to meet you, mine is Student."

"Fuckin' A, man."

Davy Boy looked proudly across the street, painting the entire Peerless building with an imaginary brush-wielding hand.

"Beautiful, ain't it?"

Across at the half-corner, the street took a dogleg to the northwest and Student could not detect beauty. Instead, he saw structural weirdness. The entire building was built on the slant and builders took advantage of this. They constructed an entire half-basement; its windows lined the sidewalks at various inclines. These were barred and screened over, in the event someone misinterpreted easy access for an invitation in. Indeed, they glowered out in a sullen aloofness.

The entrance to this basement was a yawning double door that at one time could have admitted a horse and rider into the basement. There Student saw signs — writing.

"Another hit, amigo?"

His new friend's friendly countenance changed to a snarl,

"*THIS* is where the revolution will start! Now the Ozzie and fucking Harriets are sending their sons to feed the gooks at the behest of capitalist puppets like Johnson, workers are opening their eyes. Fuckin'-A-Rights Johnny."

Student was about to take the extended bottle when he remembered past disasters plus the medications and admonishments of doctors.

He declined with thanks, telling his host of responsibilities to be at his best for an upcoming meeting. Davy Boy nodded solemn approval, withdrew the bottle and agreed,

"Righto! Keep sharp. This is a god-awful world, and it will only get worse. Good luck, amigo."

Student crossed over, walked the dozen or so feet to the cavernous basement's entrance and read — it was perhaps not festooned with signs, but it sported its share.

First off, it declared without an iota of deference to the Art Establishmentarians of the world that it was the entrance to the Butchers Town Writer's Guild — above the double doors was the acronym in hefty upper case letters made from metal, "**B.T.W.G.**"

On the bottom half of the double door —written in even larger letters than any others was the guild's motto, *"Workers of the World Kick Ass."*

Then — in a show of concern for all — on the baseboard running between the double doors and the sidewalk was a smaller sign advising, "Caution-Steps Lead Down."

There was no mention of the Haywood Playhouse within.

Yet another sign indicated to him events were not amiable; to the left of the entrance was an artless proclamation, reading, *"STAYED OUT: CLOSED Frank Fong, Owner."* Certainly Frank was one of the desperate Fong Brothers who spent time poised over the Fong hot line.

Across this, nearly obliterating it, was scrawled in audacious black graffiti, "FONG SUCKS."

And right dead center in the double doors was a hasp with no lock; below it was a metal hasp with an enormous padlock appropriate for use on the Sultan of Brunei's seraglio.

Had there been an increase in BTWG security measures? Student looked at his watch but had no watch.

Goddamn! It too had been lifted. Those two old squints were worse than Attila the Hun, save they offered a hug, which Attila would have omitted.

They skinned him to the quick in less than a minute. He was just beginning to mourn the loss of his 22 jewel watch standers wristwatch when three people walked up: One woman and two men.

Student's meeting was here.

"I'm Millicent Rothstein, this is Fred Rawley, and this august gentleman is Simon Connors; we're the Guild's Thespian Committee. You are Student Patterson, I assume?"

Student admitted such while taking in his oversight committee, surely not your garden-variety committee: Millicent Rothstein was a middle-aged crane-like woman wearing a plain black dress extending almost to her ankles. Above she wore a brownish half-open coat with a simple gray blouse. Atop all was a hat, a simple thing —with a dark ribbon around the top. She looked like a recent Salvation Army wash-out.

Fred Rawley was a smallish man — dapper with smart, if out-of-fashion, attire, and a great leprechaun smile. He extended his hand then pumped away on Student's, as if to start a flow of water from his ears. Simon Connors was the Ancient. He didn't extend his hand; rather he had serious, hawk-like eyes with matching nose. He gazed downward, then up — scanning all that was Student,

"How in hell did you come by the name of Student?"

Student told him; he rocked back on his heels somewhat; perhaps Connors liked that his parents were poor chicken farmers. Millicent Rothstein looked at Connors, and continued in an amiable tone — somewhat forced, or perhaps simply nervous.

"Mr. Conners is the President Emeritus of the Guild, so de facto member of the Thespian Committee."

"All the committees, sad to say." Connors added without smile or pride.

Rawley began a litany. He was from the "old sod"; a proud member of many socialist and progressive causes. Sweeping his hand to indicate the entirety of the Peerless Steam Beer building, added,

"I was but a young ordinary seaman when I first came here,

just before the 2nd capitalist war, I was—"

"Rawley. We had best take this inside before, watered by this rich socialist broth, we put down roots here."

Millicent Rothstein agreed affably, though Mr. President Emeritus was not affable. In fact, with great gray eyebrows he looked in a state between skeptical and resigned, a total graveyard owl.

But all three hesitated in place — Millicent effecting a sort of dainty shuffle, and Rawley looking up, around — taking a few steps to the north then south. The dour Simon Connors took out a brier pipe and pouch and began tiredly to load up.

Student knew. There was that massive lock, and someone had a massive key that fit it. Who had it? Rawley began — he had the Celtic tradition to uphold.

"Fact is, I have forgotten the key to this very formidable lock at home, and we must avail ourselves of entry via the side entrance, an awkward situation."

Simon paused in mid-motion, closed his eyes in order to summon patience, then gestured with pipe and pouch towards the door.

"Don't bullshit the man, Rawley. Fong has locked us out, Mr. Student; we're behind in the rent, and after 30 years of on-time payment, the rat-bastard has locked us out. Hell with him — we'll go over to Big Lena's. At 78 years of age, I don't climb through basement windows very well."

Millicent stopped her shuffle and looked imploringly at Student,

"This is awfully embarrassing, but Mr. Fred Fong is a terrible man, and his father has only recently passed away. A terrible loss and worse change of policy."

Rawley looked into the sky, as if the late Fong Senior would pass over, blessing them.

"Yes, he was a good person, old man Fong was."

Simon Connors would not have it.

"Well, he's dead. And that's it, and we've got to deal with that greedy eldest son of his. So let us move it along and lament later."

They led Student along, crossing back over towards his recent host and drinking companion, Davy Boy, at the base of the light pole. Seeing them approach he elevated his bottle in welcome, and Millicent initiated a group-veering from the celebrant, but it was too late.

"Milly! Goddamn! Remember Big Bill Haywood's words: Brothers and Sisters Always. KILL THE CAPITALIST COCKSUCKERS!"

In a fruitless attempt to talk over Davy Boy's presence, Millicent began a historic interpretation of the cable car tracks — or their remnant — and the social warrior was given the collective cold shoulder as they walked on and turned the corner. Student wondered if Big Bill Haywood's slogan might have benefited from additional editing.

Simon was slower than them, so Millicent stayed deferentially at the elderly man's elbow, and in fact linked arms as they strode along. Rawley eased up beside Student and sotto voce explained their sloganeering colleague.

"Davie Boy was a bit inebriated, but when sober is our staunchest guild member. I don't know where he might have gotten that bottle — awfully expensive stuff on this side of Market."

They ran into *Big Lena's All Star Café* head on. Smaller than *Artie's Eatery*, but with an entrance not requiring a gymnast's agility to enter. Considering the sour events of Student's day, the interior emanated an overall feeling of hospitality, even optimism. Several customers talked amiably at the counter.

What in hell was this congenial eatery doing amidst this desultory mass of buildings and despairing humanity?

Upon taking a booth Millicent gave a thumbnail vita of the four-foot ten Lena: Though at one time Lena could pass herself off as a midget, the International Little People Association made four-foot eight the cutoff point.

When the diminutive woman washed out of that category she became a livelong carnival and circus cook. And her history was on display — Student looked at walls festooned with carnival and circus acts of long and near past. Coming over to set them up, she saw Student admiring her wall art. Eager to interpret, she pointed to the closest with her order-pad.

"That was the original Simmons Family — sponge divers. Specialty acts like them are what really brought in the rubes."

This was a poor group — and they knew he was staying at the Mark Hopkins — so Student felt obliged to explain why he could not pick up the check.

"I would buy, but my wallet and wrist-watch were lifted this morning — as a matter of fact, just a couple of blocks from here not an hour ago."

Lena heard as did all others present — including two fellows sitting at the counter. All snapped knowing looks; their eyes spoke loudly — as if a boa constrictor hung from a light fixture.

The closest man at the counter droned,

"Were they two long-in-the-tooth hags — looked like old toads; work one at the side and one in front?"

Student's face said it all. The elder Simon shook his head and put his pipe down.

"One thing Mr. Student — south of Market — you worry less about flowers in your hair and more about creatures like those two misfits of femininity — they are a more effective criminal combo than if Mata-Hari and Carmen teamed up."

"I'll see what I can do, Simon."

The speaker slid off his stool and left, shaking his head. Millicent checked her purse, and made an attempt at cheerful fellowship,

"I think we can use coffee all the way around, and a sinker for me, and anyone else who would like that."

While Millicent reviewed the plans and future of the Haywood Playhouse, Student's internal conductor and brakeman on his *Basic Survival Railroad* tossed out red lanterns and tightened up the brakes: He added up the bad-omens of the morning and decided at once on an exit strategy. Even if plans for the Haywood Playhouse included a grand opening with Lawrence Olivier and Richard Burton debuting a recently discovered tragedy by Shakespeare, Student was history. This collection of lame-brained, anachronistic Never-Weres and Has-Beens added up to the most catastrophic graduate program in long history of colleges and universities.

If needs be, he would hitchhike back to Iowa and raise chickens.

The following day, Student found solace and understanding at the Graduate School offices.

The Dean of the Graduate School offered him shelter: He guaranteed Student a home in the college's regular English Department.

"Mr. Patterson, your record and scores don't come by this institution every day. Just brave it out a few more weeks, and I shall fix the matter."

Student didn't think his transcripts were *that* good, but he did know that colleges were hurting for good Ph.D. candidates.

College departments swelled with young men averse to

participating in a lame brained war directed by like-minded leaders — so these institutions enjoyed banner recruitment by their graduate schools. These choice hideouts inflated like air bladders with those whose idea of *The Dawn Patrol* was a stiff Saturday night drunk.

But the draft boards wised up. Hapless potential draftees were flushed from shelter becoming vulnerable before the Gods of War.

This Dean, the wormy sort occupying all administrations, was secure about Student's sense of duty contrasted with the present crop of whiners and love children populating campuses in the fall of 1968.

Student knew waiting would have its advantages.

4.

His section of English composition was an honor's section, a posh assignment. This meant fewer and better quality essays to grade, and even better, it would end four weeks early. He deserved it after the college sent him to a fleecing in Butchertown.

Student could wait around a month or three for a "home" in the complicated world of graduate school mechanisms. He had his monthly fellowship income, his military benefits, so screw Jenkins and his Butchertown Crow Bait.

"I would like to know why I got a "B" on my essay."

His smug reverie was destroyed by Miss Exception-To-The-Rules: She was the *First* caller of his *First* session of office hours — her visit subsequent to his returning the *First* essay at the end of the *First* week of classes.

"Because, Miss ah, ah . . ."

"Bolton. Jessica Bolton."

"Yes, Miss Bolton. Well, for the first assignment, it was a good essay, so I gave it a B."

"If it is good, why is it a B?"

"Because it is not superior or excellent, which is an A."

"Why not?" Realizing she was a tad abrupt, she started over, "I mean, Professor Patterson. Why not?"

During graduate school and in the Navy Rating College he had enjoyed the hundreds of respectful students. Though she was officially a senior, this was a freshman class. Undergraduates of any stripe kept their place and didn't ask such saucy questions.

Student remembered Miss Bolton's desire to save 10 bucks and slip under the guard rail free of charge and effort.

He didn't like her. During the first three classes she asked too many questions and dressed like a janitress in a meat packing plant. Now she showed up bitching about a goddamned B.

Another annoying side to her was she possessed a strange atmosphere of sexuality. Student knew well she controlled and operated this mechanism as necessity dictated, which was now — when she wanted him to kick her grade up a full notch.

He liked her even less.

But one didn't argue with one's students; they dwelled beneath the salt, and he above it: He began and ended his litany seamlessly: It was a B. This was a good grade, even more so for an honor's section. There were 10 weeks of classes remaining and many more opportunities for a writer of her ambitions.

End of story. Goodbye and . . . please feel free to come again for any reason.

He did not mean that, of course — he hoped she was angry enough to drop his course. She left in something of a minor huff. Well, huff or no — this Bolton woman was strictly over her head in a college. He knew.

Also this incident was a good launch upon the proving ground for his program of informed misogyny. And why not?! It had come upon him — spawned by eight years of emotional investment in a woman who flushed him down the toilet into the city's settlement ponds.

We'll see who goes down whose toilet.

"Worn and frumpy, but surprisingly erect breasts on her. Mature ones are better at sex, too."

It was Dr. Jenkins. He slipped into Student's office — leaned back out to look again down the corridor at a retreating Miss Bolton, then came in,

Jenkins' appraisal of her was sure as hell not his — Student braced himself for a fully acrimonious encounter.

Jenkins had the same chewed-on briefcase, but someone

had rendered his right eye orbit a deep blue; his scalp sported a bandage, and the hand holding his briefcase was likewise dressed, and one wrist swollen. He followed Student's eyes, then shrugged — the nonchalant gesture of the hardened gladiator.

"They're getting desperate. Busted us up, the sons-of-bitches. But we made all the final editions."

His fingers drummed his briefcase; was he preoccupied with matters of war? But at once he snapped back to business,

"You know, Student, I would have appreciated it if you expressed worries to me about the Butchertown Writer's Guild before you did to that overgrown hemorrhoid Marston. As a military sort, you should know about following the chain of command."

"The secretary told me you were in jail."

"True enough, but she hates me. Long story."

Jenkins took Student in a surprise flank attack beginning not with anger but sympathy: He understood how a graduate student after being robbed then locked out on the first day might sour on the project.

"But Student, you must be resolute; otherwise, how might scholars survive? Here you have a generous stipend for three years, a place to live, half-off, and a chance to observe and — and — participate in the renewal of one of the prime folk icons in the western United States."

Student wasn't ready for the heartfelt approach, and finessed a response. He wasted ineffectual words about his ambition and dreams while Jenkins put his foot upon the edge of his chair, reached under the cuff and took out a flask,

"Brandy? Strictly ancient stuff."

Student declined while Jenkins took a gentlemanly hit and returned the vessel to its place.

"Yes, Student. I know you are ambitious. So, listen to this

voice of experience. You'll want a damned good place when you are done here. And look at the originality of both the work and the research. My God, there won't be a recently hatched Ph.D. anywhere that could match your resume."

When Jenkins had gotten through with him, he naively agreed to give the situation a longer trial period before resigning his fellowship; also, in an even unlikelier deal, he agreed to talk to Millicent Rothstein one more time — at the Guild Hall.

"She is very sorry about the first meeting. Actually Miss Rothstein is an interesting intellectually committed woman, even if she does have hairy legs."

Then Jenkins asked how his honors class was proceeding — a presumptive inquiry — then departed.

Student's spirits sank after this failure of resolve. He began to doubt his instincts. Prior to this his social instruments were fine-tuned by the rightness of American normalcy. There was over a decade of Debbie's undying love, loyalty — and more than anything, purpose. Above all, plans were absolutely a must for normalcy.

But Debbie's blast-off to the planet of Whoopee — and who knows what else — had caught him flat-footed. She had flown off into the unknown, the ultimate silly goose.

Student sensed something uncommon was also coming straight at him and he wanted to be gone before it hit. His suspicions revolved around Jenkins, for he was not vaguely similar to any other college professor he had, and certainly not any superior officers in the navy.

Student went on red-alert, marooned in a weird land composed of confusion and by a code of Devil Take the Hindmost. Normalcy and marital devotion had vaporized in brimstone and self-interest.

5.

Seers of Future Present

(Elder Men and Women dressed as Father and Mother Time, women sans beards)

Flee Student! Get thee back to your family's chickens and feed corn. You are being ingested by that great whale-shark, the American Academic Circle Jerk. In this world there are no friends, good fellowship, or kindnesses. Women and men fight over degrees as spotted hyenas do baboon carcasses. On top of that, your country is busy giving itself oral sex in Southeast Asia and the upheaval of it has spread onto campuses nation-wide.

And we have even grimmer news.

Dark forces, The Ancient Crones whose proper name we don't dare speak, have decided to make life miserable for you because you have affronted womankind. But we are doing our best to represent you. We'll have a better chance with you in Iowa hiding in the feed corn.

So, flee Student, escape the voracious maw of this dreadful monstrosity sucking you in like so much pasta. And if you fail to do so, don't say we didn't tell you.

6.

"Student, I think we should have sex straight away, and get through the petty bourgeois barrier that impedes creativity between men and women."

It was not developing into your normal Sunday. Student had walked to the Butchertown Writer's Guild hall from a more reasonably priced hotel right in the middle of downtown San Francisco — a half block from Market Street.

He had decided a deal was a deal, to give the matter a polite forty-eight hours then formally withdraw from Jenkins' world of madness.

But first he must meet Milly Rothstein.

She waited for him at the entrance, hairy legs and all.

The padlock was off the basement doors, and Milly was alone. She started with a general tour of the guild hall that years before was the shipping and receiving area of Peerless Steam Beer.

The floor was constructed of planks stout enough to support a massive wagon and a team-of-six. The BTWG actually took up only one half of this basement area; the entire sub-floor was nearly half the size of a football field.

"Many hundreds-of-thousand gallons of beer passed through here,"she said with a sigh, adding, "with workers sweating themselves to nothing for a few cents an hour, of course."

The Haywood Playhouse was in ruins. The stage and seating area were torn asunder during the great *Lower Depths* opening night riot in 1958.

Milly had been there — the set designer and one of the players.

"FBI agent provocateurs of course caused it — or started it. That was the death knell of that season and all subsequent seasons." She turned, gestured — arms apart, fingers extended, "Now it will all change. This is what the grant from the *Institute of Northern Reprisal* shall revitalize, Mr. Patterson. Fifty thousand dollars is an unbelievable windfall. I'm so optimistic. My older sister Peggy was totally responsible for it; she is such a soldier for the cause."

She reassured him of the artistic and professional merit of the project — and especially with his addition to it via the contract the institute had signed with the college.

While he gazed around at broken boards, old benches in splinters — cobwebs and dust mice accumulated since 1958, she took off her coat. Beneath it wasn't the black dress of mourning she had on before, but a knit knee-length affair.

It was then she made her statement about the clarity needed between men and women involved in creative endeavors.

This was a low-light situation in black and white, and Student knew full well the woman was old enough to be his mother or close to it — if his mother had had powerful hormones.

"I don't know what to say, Miss Rothstein."

"We are about to have sex, so I think you can call me Milly."

She took him by the arm and led him in the direction of the guild office. In back was a smallish room divided from the whole by a blanket with a woven illustration of an Indian sitting in classic style, smoking a cigar rather than a peace pipe. Above him was the trademark "Big Chief Stogies."

Student wasn't being dragged, nor was he scooting along with great anticipation. The Socialist theorist, practitioner and femme fatale flicked on a small light, and against the wall was a neatly made iron cot, ready to go.

"Sometimes the others or I sleep here if we suspect Mr.

Fong is going to lock us out."

"I've only recently recovered my health, Milly."

"I understand."

She shed her dress and shoes in a simple shrug and two-step, and indeed she had hairy legs. But she also had a slender figure that would have knocked models in the *New Yorker* on their semi-emaciated buttocks.

All of Milly's most vital prominences were present and none belonged or were resident on his mother.

If décor and condition equated to distance, his move to the *A plus B Hotel*, two blocks from the guild hall, was as drastic if he had jumped ship in Kuala Lumpur.

But the *A plus B* rent was one-half off as part of Student's fellowship.

The bedraggled hotel clung to dereliction as a trail donkey might the rim of the Grand Canyon. It was a second floor walkup meaning that the layers of the hotel — in this case five, began on the 2nd floor. These did not need elevators; evidently the City of Saint Francis's code-makers believed in exercise for elders, the semi-infirm and inebriates.

Student was never into fine living — or even modest lounging. Anywhere to lie down was good enough, and room number seven at the *A plus B Hotel* met that requirement with a few millimeters to spare.

The day before the move, Miss Ruth Smith, resident manager, fawned over Student when she checked him in.

"Oh, Professor Patterson we are so thrilled to have you. Aren't we Eddy?"

"Damned straight."

Her one-armed live-in, a former teamster, grunted

agreement, eyes remaining fixed on the tiny-screened TV. It was roller derby time on Channel Five.

Miss Smith's haunches rolled from starboard to port as she maneuvered up the stairs to the 3rd floor, and showed him to number seven. The carpets along the 3rd floor corridor showed signs of eternal siege — burns, unrecognizable smudges, sly patch jobs, and 100,000 mile wear rendered the original design as difficult to discern as ancient tatters found in Persian tombs.

Lining the corridor were buckets painted red and half-full of sand meant for cigarette butts, but were used for other purposes with distressing clarity.

Over each room's door was a light, intended decades before as night illumination but small flame-shaped bulbs were burned out, broken or gone. A few of the fixtures themselves were removed, leaving loose wires dangling.

"This is my best room Professor. Sort of a studio, like Gene Kelley used in *American in Paris*, I mean, that was such a good, wholesome movie. Eddy and I have no use for these modern dirty movies. Plus, it is on the fire escape. I never give this to bums, too easy for them to jump rent."

Taking her master key from a ribbon around her neck, she opened number seven. The room exhaled a burst of Lysol Cleaner and Kill-All bug spray that momentarily caused Student's knees to gelatinize.

He braced himself by putting a supporting arm to the door jamb,

"You must pardon the smell, Professor; I cleaned this room especially well — or rather Eddy did — he didn't open the window. Here."

It was indeed a large window, and thrown open — with the hearty cross-ventilation created by the open door — it expelled enough fumes to flush the resident pigeons on the fire escape, sending them gasping.

She completed a room tour within a minute: There was a sink, a bed, a table with chair, a small bureau, and a shy little nightstand next to a double bed, itself of a metal frame, in faux brass, including claws for each of the four legs.

One light hung from a wire in the middle of the room; and a single plug was between the bed and basin.

"The toilet and shower are at the end of the hall, and I keep them absolutely clean, Professor — you can depend on it."

When he moved in on a Sunday afternoon he stuck his head in the open half of the door finding Eddy was asleep in an easy chair. There was no sign of Miss Smith.

The taxi driver had paused when he told him his destination, and gave him an extra-once over. Like his entire brotherhood, he was alert for deadbeats with deadbeat destinations.

Eddy had submerged into his sheep-counting mode and Student paused, allowing his arms to rest from carrying his burden up the stairs to the third floor.

Voices from behind informed that a weighty topic was underway.

"Listen Mr. Estes, I've told you before, and I won't again. No peeing in the basin. If you can't make the john, use a can and dump it in the toilet later."

Miss Smith was down the hall repeating a cardinal rule of the establishment; the lecture came from a second floor room. Student learned later these were inferior to third and fourth floor rooms. Miss Smith put questionable tenants on the second floor for reasons of increased scrutiny.

Rent jumpers being the worst sorts.

She returned to the office shaking her head in professional

frustration, saw Student, and at once brightened.

"Oh! Professor Patterson, you're moving in."

She praised him, passed through her door, and handed him the key. Student noted she glanced at Eddy with a tad of scorn, then returned her attentions to welcoming Student: She commenced an oft recited list of the positives regards living at the *A plus B Hotel,* editing past the negatives.

These included proximity to all the stores and cafes in the area, and most of the favored taverns. Many she claimed were historical structures going back to — but not beyond — the great San Francisco Earthquake and Fire of 1906.

"Save for the Peerless Building. Lots of history there. Even experts can't explain how it ever stood up — owners didn't even make repairs."

Hiking up to his room, Student put both suitcases on the floor next to his bed, opened the window again, and sat down. In addition to all else the *entire* guild hall might collapse mid-act.

It just all overwhelmed.

Every one of his joints ached, or so it seemed. Having sex with Millicent Rothstein roared to that with any of the dozens of professional girls at Mother Lee's bordello in Saigon. In fact, by now Student felt confident enough to compare sex with Milly as being in a full-throated typhoon, versus riding out the weather along moderate to mild seas at Mother Lees.

Milly decided their once-a-week "artistic meetings" also include a hearty screwing in the guild hall's watch stander's cot, or in fact anytime there was a tasteful opportunity. She challenged even progressive views.

"Student, it is only through the orgasm that women may attain true and absolute liberation from capitalist society.

They can never be shy of them. Edna St. Vincent Millay knew this. Her enlightened views have been suppressed by male dominated forces."

Milly was helping Student travel towards that same enlightened point even though male. Her physical drive was impressive. Milly could not have weighed much over a hundred pounds.

"I am overly strong for my build," she would explain while soothing a spent Student with a moist towel.

When he, with sincere mortification, related his previous education to Milly, she lamented the plight of women the world over.

"The poor things. I can only imagine."

In the more high-profile districts of San Francisco, free love and alike were the banner-headlines at first regionally and now internationally. Nowhere would one read about the Butchertown district. Student and Milly, however, by screwing away determinedly in the bowels of the old brewery culturally linked the sagging spirit of this area to more colorful districts. They too proclaimed *Love The One You're With,* and other cultural directives.

It was the week before Freddy O'Malley, Millicent Rothstein's main man and favorite actor, was released from Federal prison. She wanted to greet Freddy fully starved for healthy revolutionary sex, so Student was gently removed from her slate indefinitely.

Rather than regretting this, Student experienced philosophical growth, seeing it as a step forward. He and Milly had actually gotten other things done, including planning a late spring season opener at a reconstructed Haywood Playhouse.

The Haywood Playhouse would courageously resume where they let off, with Maxim Gorky's *The Lower Depths*. It was the overwhelmingly sentimental favorite for Milly Rothstein and the entire Guild, or what remained of them.

For Student, God was great or very close to it. Life was easing up, and the best thing was to operate without well-defined, ambitious plans. Was not a plan itself a pitfall?

His only class in composition was a teacher's dream: being an honor's section, the essays were good with the exception of the frumpy Miss Bolton. She presumed to get creative and forgo formal compositional protocols, and in true academic tradition her grade took it in the hind end.

She would show up and make a fuss, but the hell with her — Student had other concerns; the first priority was not whether to get a car or not, but what sort of car? Without a future including a house with pricey Dutch doors and faux ebony counters he had healthy savings and war bonds purchased by his parents.

Student, in the interest of proletariat modesty, would eschew a make or model that would brand him economically. He must maintain an egalitarian profile to match his new scholarly residence in Butchers Town.

He decided to dine on the issue.

When on the state college-end of the city, Student often supped in a nearby pizza joint.

On his way he once again noticed ground wisps of tear gas pocketed in low places. He had developed an eye and nose for time elapsed and knew the fracas was well over. Only a numskull would disregard the chaos of writhing crowds, warring protesters, cops and grasping media.

In truth, scenes like these challenged Student with an impossibility: He could not visualize even the 'new' Debbie, goggles tightened, bandanna around her hair, sandals and long skirt, hurling words and even more substantial objects at police.

Then, when the mêlée ended, rushing into nearby shrubbery and copulating — humping away with a hirsute male like energized poodles.

He grew tired of wrestling with this conundrum and soon was enjoying his privacy and poring over car ads in the classifieds. His hair was now long enough to enjoy group approval. Pizza was a contrast to Butchers Town where he was developing a taste for the fare at *Big Lena's All Star Café.*

An authoritative baritone voice pulled his attention from the ads.

"Are you Student Patterson?"

He was looking at a police badge.

"I'm Sergeant Porter, SFPD, this here is my partner Inspector Stark." They slid in, one next to him, the Sergeant across. Student knew at once this visit had Professor Jenkins written both on the front and rear of it. No doubt the bastard had used him as an alibi.

He put down the newspaper and a slice of pizza and prepared himself.

"You teach composition, right?"

This was an odd shot to the chops. Student sensed what a trapped rat might the instant the bail zipped overhead to bash his brains out.

"Yes."

"And one of your students is Jessica Bolton, right?

"Yes"

The sergeant's partner saw need of input.

"I like this guy, Sarge; he's an agreeable son-of-a-bitch."

"Shut up, Jimmy," he leaned across, digging his eyes into Student's "Mr. Student I hear you're sort of an arrogant asshole."

"Who in fuck would name a guy Student?"

"I said, shut up, Jimmy. Let the guy respond. We want to be fair."

Student was scrambling just to make sense out of an inexplicable development.

"I don't understand. What is the police department's concern with my freshman English class?"

Jimmy-The-Cop gave up on witty interjections, drew Student's pizza over, and began consuming it, including pieces of crust Student abandoned.

"The concern is this, *Mr. Student*: She is my fiancée, and I come home expecting peace and calm and a little care and attention." Here the partner raised his forearm level with the table, and making a fist, pumped it back and forth several times. Even with a mouth full he was a classic Shakespearean clown.

". . . so, instead I listen to shit about essays and her asshole teacher, and her being the best writer in any class he ever had before this. And this fucker stiffing her with lousy grades, and me getting more and more cold, you might say, without a little warmth and attention because of this goddamned essay or English class," and he reached over and neat as a blink, plucked the top button from Student's shirt and shot it across the aisle to the next booth, fortunately empty. ". . . So I'm getting sick of listening to her, and I'm here to make sure it doesn't happen anymore. Do you understand, you sorry son-of-a-bitch?"

Student understood the gorilla's mission; he looked down at his undershirt peeping out from its new-found freedom.

At this critical instant, Student experienced an epiphany — life changing, without doubt. He no longer cared about normalcy, abnormalcy, or in point of fact much at all. The exceptions were healthy proletariat sex, chicken fried steak at Big Lena's and the possibility of directing *The Lower Depths* for the second and greatest opening at the *Haywood Playhouse.*

He didn't care about himself anymore or at least with causes that were all *his.* This certainly included a doctorate degree or any degrees. The policemen did not enjoy pauses for epiphanies.

"Just don't sit there with your face hanging out, pecker head; *do you understand?*"

Student stared into this set of bestial eyes attached via primitive circuitry to the creature's fists and penis. Student was conversing with a walking, talking sexual organ.

"You know, sergeant, I think I do but don't care. Miss Bolton gets what she gets, and what you say or do has nothing — will have nothing — to do with it."

The comedian stopped in mid-swallow, eyes opened and looked with mawkish disbelief at his opposite. The old Sarge withdrew an iota, as if sniffing something foul, then as outrageous affront seeped through his hide he reached over to grab a handful of Student.

"Ok, you miserable fuck, let me be more —"

"Friends, have you taken Jesus for your personal savior?"

The cops looked up at two young men — both holding bibles and a stack of handouts. Their eyes glowed with eternal truth. They wore long collarless shirts with glowing designs and trousers festooned with calico patches. And more than anything, their appearances were grandly topped with bushels and pecks of bristling hair.

They were Jesus People — Student encountered mention of them in several of his classes' essays. Lately they enjoyed a strong press presence for their accomplishments as public nuisances.

The sergeant reached deeply into his public self and managed,

"Take a powder. This is police business."

And badged them when they remained.

His partner then swallowed the remains of Student's pizza before managing, "He means get lost," then mumbled a street-grade negative about 'Jesus Freaks.'

"I'm sorry, but you cannot show Jesus your badge and least of all say, 'Get lost' to Our Savior who loves us all."

Sarge took his eyes from Student — they narrowed and he thumbed towards the door,

"Get the hell gone before you piss me off and I bust you both for interfering."

The Jesus People wavered, for like most their tribe they were recent converts to the movement and well-remembered jails, arrests, and institutional food.

"Ooooooooink! Oohhhh, Piggy!"

This vocalization came from the central area of the pizzeria — a seating area with tables and chairs. The perimeter was booths and doorways, then the kitchen/oven area. The central area was occupied by well over thirty customers — all from the college.

The two cops failed to realize that when police authorities beat students to a jelly at protests and demonstrations, it was unwise to visit their victims' favorite eateries where close to forty students harboring grudges occupied a confined space. Such spaces were excellent for throwing.

"Oooooooooooooink, ooooooooooooooooink, pig, pig piggy!"

The Jesus People demonstrated keen perception and cleared out fast.

The pizza-hungry cop jumped up and yelled, "We got ourselves some fucking comedians here, Sarge. Some real farm hands."

A rash soul did a wonderful rendition of another porcine grunt, followed by a realistic oink. The Sarge got up and stood, shifting his trousers, preparing to deliver a drubbing. He looked down threateningly at Student.

"Stay put, asshole. I'll finish with you after these piss ants."

He turned to the group, reached under his coat and drew out a set of handcuffs. This veteran law enforcer took no guff from anyone.

"Which of you faggot, draft evading motherfuckers wants to be first? The guys downtown love booking pig-imitators."

A volunteer signaled his — or possibly her — hesitation to go downtown by launching one of the establishment's glass beer pitchers at the Sarge.

"Watch it, Sarge!"

Action: The throw was accurate, aimed at the sergeant's skull. He ducked as quickly as boxer might an overhand right, allowing the vessel to shatter against a wall, spraying shrapnel everywhere.

Out came the inspector's gun.

"OK, get your fucking hands up where we can see them."

At the same moment the owner, usually a jolly man named Larry, came running out sweeping his apron off.

"What in the hell is going on here, God damnit!?"

The owner's entry coincided with a second launch, this time a beer stein which the owner sidestepped with practiced ease. Jimmy-The-Cop fired his weapon into the ceiling; the muzzle blast illuminated the faux grapevines — the place's décor — sending a length of it across Student's table.

Officially Student occupied the Vietnam conflict zone intermittently for almost one year without seeing a shot fired. Even as this action went potentially lethal, this irony did not escape him.

Bedlam ruled.

The hostile students did not thrust hands in the air or stand their ground but hauled ass for the exit or got low to the floor level and began a rifle-range crawl. The owner bellowed in outrage, and Student — seeing he was free to slide from the booth, did so, naturally staying out of the line of fire.

The two policemen were busy trying to cuff a man to a chair while his girlfriend screamed invectives.

Reaching up and snagging his well-marked classified section, Student exited via the rear door. He had marked a half dozen cars, but he was most interested in the little convertible MG. The issue was, would that be a show of class-insensitivity? Still, he always wanted one of them.

The day following the fiasco Student sat in his office considering earlier advice: At the *A plus B Hotel*, in a rare move towards verbosity, Eddy advised student against a convertible,

"Down here, they'll cut through the top and take every damned thing," and he continued, advising against Student's next choice, a station wagon, ". . . you'll go out and find two or three people living in it," and in fact a car in general, ". . . where you going to park it? It'll run you a mint in just parking meter fees."

In fact, Eddy's advice was the sanest, up to a point: With the public transportation being so good it paid to use it. If and when, Eddy continued, you desperately needed a car, you could boost one in less than a half hour.

But Student, though, liked to go on wandering drives — it is how you learned an area, and he felt more comfortable in his own car.

He was opening up the day's classifieds to look again, when an attractive woman entered his office. Her looks were so stunning, if he had lacked strength-of-resolution, his plans for misogyny would have endured a helluva dent. Yet when she put a drop slip on his desk, he looked up into the unmistakable intense eyes of Miss Jessica Bolton.

It was as if he'd witnessed a noxious green caterpillar turn to a butterfly. She looked up momentarily — perhaps to grasp necessary but uncharacteristic words, then switched large blue eyes back to Student.

"I'm awfully sorry for what happened. He told me."

Student slid his newspaper away, and swam around in his own confusion before securing traction.

"I'm surprised your fiancé said anything, frankly."

"What! " she fell back a pace, ". . . he's not my fiancé. And he's not anything to me anymore after what he pulled. He's a drunk."

The drop slip was a symbol of great relief, anything that would say good riddance to her. She shrugged,

"I learned a lesson . . . I hope I can get my full time job back at I. Magnum's; I'll need it to pay rent. So, I won't be able to go to school anyway."

He had nothing to say to a woman whose taste for sexual scum nearly got him beaten senseless. Student briskly swept the drop slip over, fished out a pen, yet a grim thought occurred,

"What assurance do I have that animal friend of yours isn't lurking about waiting for me somewhere, not that I care that much. I don't yield to thuggery."

"He is *not* my friend. Anyway, I told him if he bothered you . . . well, I have enough on him to get him fired and prosecuted, so not to worry Professor Patterson."

He signed.

"I wish you luck in future educational endeavors."

"No you don't."

She turned and left. So Miss Jessica Bolton concluded with typical insolence. Student took comfort he would never see her again, especially if he remembered not to browse at I. Magnums

7.

Seers of Future Present
(Elder Men and Women dressed as shepherds)

Student, we have returned from the tranquil slopes of Mount Olympus. We warn you, that you are now affronting both Artemis and Aphrodite with this misogyny fiddle faddle. You have done nothing to patch up your outrage of the Ancient Ones; instead have turned your back both on the concept of family and passion. Hence we have divined that you are putting yourself in the hapless position of becoming a classic ruminant in the headlights. You are making our task tough sledding indeed.

At least remember your mother and father for Christmas, you are going to need them.

Held a week before Christmas, the Butchertown Writer's Guild secular gathering was without holiday décor of any sort. If a person were historically challenged at meetings of the Butchertown Writer's Guild they were lost souls. The period 1900-1968 was to members recent news. Victories and defeats to the socialist labor movement in, say 1935, were discussed like last week's ball scores.

Attendees regarded political victories as a hybrid between

icons and mother's milk. They bandied about names of politicians long dead — especially those held in loathing — as evangelicals might horned demons or witches with fiery hair. And more than anything, the anti-war movement was a naive dimple on the fatted posterior of capitalism.

Officially and actually, this year's meeting was a dual affair marking the complete re-construction of the Haywood Playhouse. Also, it was a welcome home party marking the release from prison of their prominent member Freddy O'Malley, who enjoyed the moniker of the "Dunsmuir Bomber."

Freddy was a massive man. When he wrapped his arm around Millicent, he dwarfed her. Student felt his eyes upon him and feared that if Milly had not kept their socialist exercises confidential he was in dicey waters.

But this ominous possibility was overcome by the convivial ambiance. In fact Student was sure he was seeing virtually all the living or non-incarcerated members of the guild in one place.

The FBI and ATF (Bureau of Alcohol, Tobacco, Firearms, and Explosives) each assigned a team who observed from opposite sides of the Peerless Steam beer building in unmarked cars that looked precisely like unmarked cars.

"The Feds are in great attendance, people!!"

And when old Simon Conners — President Emeritus — announced the presence of outside guests, there was a rise of cheerful jeers, throaty boos and a sprinkle of obscenities and profanities, with the concluding topper,

"Kill the Capitalist Cocksuckers!"

Davie Boy Watkins didn't need strong drink to shout his favorite slogan of defiance and disdain, though it helped.

There *were* three and a half things outlawed in all meetings by guild caveat: Firearms, bomb making material, or worse an actual bomb — with alcohol coming in an ambiguous fourth.

These rules avoided their greatest bugbears of Federal law. Not on a few occasions warrants were served and searches undertaken during gatherings — a pro-forma mark of disapproval.

The Feds learned in the early years not to be caught napping by such societal misanthropes as the BTWG.

Student saw, however, that though prohibiting alcohol made sense there were occasional lapses here and there. Considering the present mix of political views — excessive drink might ignite into ugliness. The attendee's beliefs varied from the not-too-unorthodox radical members of the Democratic Party, to full blossomed teeth-clenching ideologues of the Communist Workers League. This latter group considered themselves the elite of American radicalism.

"American Socialists are bourgeois romantics, and have been cleaning up turds after the elephants pass since 1895. Only by outright Marxist/Leninism can we kick serious ass."

Yes, surely it was not a single-doctrine crowd.

He overheard many more social conversations while threading his way to the refreshments. Even Jenkins was there, and Student was surprised — not surprised? — [he could not decide] when he recognized Jenkins' escort. She was the young lady who threatened to cast herself from the golden gate bridge in the minutes preceding his first formal meeting with the Jenkins. It never occurred to Student that his major professor was the heel whose predations drove her into despair.

But — maybe he was being unfair to his Chairman: Perhaps she was a recent social addition, and Jenkins was showing her the intellectual positives of remaining alive. Certainly her presence was appreciated: Two male Guild stalwarts ignored Jenkins instead staring at her breasts lurking under a loose-weave sweater. Consistent with social frankness between the genders, the member with a perfect Lenin beard observed,

"You have the most voluptuous breasts on the planet, young lady. Do you attend socialist functions regularly?"

This abrupt compliment caused her to giggle, redden and Jenkins to raise his eyebrows. Student's eagerness to see this vignette play out was interrupted.

"So you're going to direct *Depths?*"

Student looked at — then up — at the towering Freddy O'Malley, recently of Federal confinement for first degree possession of bomb making material. He stuck out his hand and saw it disappear in O'Malley's paw.

"I will."

O'Malley looked down at Student with a gaze he did not associate with a liberated view towards healthy proletariat sex. Again he hoped to God Milly had been discreet.

O'Malley put aside his cup of punch, raised a friendly hand to his shoulder and gave him a reassuring pat,

"I hear good things about you from Milly. You'll see me front and center at the casting call. When will it be, anyway?"

"Oh, I am so sorry I have not introduced you two before this."

Milly came over and Student could not help but stare — she wore a form-fitting dress that successfully made her look almost attractive, including the two prominent pelvic bulges and the sudden under-curve of her abdomen as it sloped towards regions of sensual concern.

Student began to suffer bourgeois manifestations from her presence. In view of O'Malley's proximity this showed a lack of timing and propriety.

He tried mightily to concentrate on the precise date and time of his casting call when the Fates intervened.

"OK, we got visitors."

It was the Guild's Sergeant of arms, Davy Boy; four Feds

came down the stairs, and one held up a warrant,

"FBI. We have a search warrant for the premises. "

"Well, La-De-Fucking-Da."

This speck of disrespect was proffered by the recent Federal graduate, Freddy O'Malley. But shuffling in front of him — interceding in his official capacity was President Emeritus Simon Conners who took the warrant, was about to open and read it when a fifth agent entered.

He was a veteran, older than the others and apparently in charge. He smoked a pipe, and confronted Conners with a slight bow, making himself comfortable on the corner of a table. With feigned good fellowship he greeted his old adversary,

"Well, it's the Old Celtic Fellow Traveler, Simon Conners. Simon! How is your health?"

Groans emanated from most attendees. Conners appraised the agent, starting at his shoes and working his way up to the hat.

"Agent Baker. It has been a few years. I thought you retired, perhaps to a profitable bail bond shop in Vegas. You would do well there."

Agent Baker was Student's first real-life FBI, and with his four man team, that made five all at once in one place. It dawned on Student — and dawned was the most accurate verb — that the Butchertown Writer's Guild was peopled by those who just didn't talk a militant game nor profess the blessings of non-violence.

One of the agents opened an attaché case with a snap and a twirl, and handed his supervisor a fat manila envelope. Senior agent Baker pulled out a crisp photographic anthology of diverse guild members.

"Oh, here it is: Wonderful portraits of all you Reds, each one brings back fond memories to me, they surely do." He extended the first to O'Keefe, "This is you O'Keefe, AKA the Dunsmuir

Bomber? Your release agreement stated you should not mix with any revolutionary dinosaurs I now find you with. Here is a great photo of you doing just that, yesterday, and of course right now."

"I have a constitutional right to free association, Baker. I served my time so you stick that photograph up President Johnson's ass. I'd say Director Hoover's, but he'd enjoy it."

The four agents who'd been busy searching what passed for the Guild's office stood bolt upright. Loyal to the letter — upon hearing their pioneer leader and founder so insulted, they were about to retaliate. Agent Baker held up his hand for patience.

That was as far as this hostile encounter, and trash-talking went—

—When the blast occurred, Agent Baker was sent tumbling backwards to the floor. Long accumulated dust trickled down from the first-floor beams above the basement level flouring everyone like a raw batch of chicken legs. Millicent, the young lady with Jenkins, and several others managed great outcry.

In reflecting back a few days after the blast Student remembered a few Guild members made no reaction at all. Rather they stood bolt still, and could he recall a slip of a smile on O'Keefe's face? Perhaps not.

However a non-member, like Jenkins — oft cop-beaten and gassed — dropped to the floor, yelling, "Take Cover!"

The professor's reaction time was surprisingly faster than the much younger Federal agents who belly dived to the planks, yet in the first seconds of the aftermath, they leaped back up, running courageously towards the entrance, guns drawn, as did Agent Baker, who shouted back to the party attendees,

"This is a crime scene; nobody leave!"

Members, of course, paid little mind, but filed out to view the scene. Student was confronted with an urgent Jenkins — he towed his now weeping young lady behind . He grabbed Student by the elbow and warned, "Student, since we represent the university, we should haul ass."

And he continued his hasty exit — switching the girl to the front to break trail, as it were, pushing her shopping cart style . Student, not driven cynical by years of militant protests, thought running from a crime scene would surely raise suspicion. He stayed, following others outside.

All confronted a wondrous aftermath: Though the explosion was loud, the engine block of the FBI's car appeared to have been the victim of master engine thieves who'd extracted the stout mechanism with hand tools. Yet the engine was very much still there. The only give-a-way that its launch from under the hood had *not* been mechanical was like an iron-clad giant grasshopper, it had come back down, landing on the vehicle's roof, creating an ugly crater.

The grill, headlights and such were not only intact, but seemingly unscathed, and the hoses and wires hung from the engine compartment, like blood vessels pulled clear.

Davy Boy threaded between Guild members, warning them to stay distant,

"Stay away everyone. Don't get the good stuff on you — otherwise you'll test positive."

O'Malley pointed out the professionalism of the operation.

"Even Bomber Rothstein himself would be hard pressed to do work that clean. Jesus, that is nice placement; it's like a crew of Mexicans cut the engine out."

Millicent demurred at the mention of her iconic father — the greatest pyrotechnical engineer in the early labor movement. His activities were in the forefront of the more radical branches of radical labor movement. Finally in early 1945 the master designer was given full time recognition within Federal housing.

The chaos of arriving fire wagons offered Student a

distraction, and he decided to withdraw. He learned later it was but another two or three minutes that arrests began, first and foremost were O'Malley and Davy Boy, journeymen pyrotechnics and former apprentices of Bomber Rothstein. Then poor Milly, for no other reason than she was Bomber Rothstein's daughter.

Student read in next day's newspapers that the resumes of his co-attendees at the Haywood Playhouse were hardly those of cranks.

The heavy hitters of the Butchertown Writer's Guild drew the most press: O'Malley had diverse arrests and one conviction, all dealing with explosives. Davy Boy and his incarcerated wife ran afoul of the ATF and other agencies by violating laws pertaining to *'controlled compounds.'* The guild's President Emeritus, Simon Conners was involved — if not led — the infamous labor upheavals during the Ford Motor Company Starvation Riot of 1932, and Memorial Day Massacre of 1937. He continued to play pivotal parts in labor conflicts since that time.

But most alarmist ink was spent on those "*. . . former students of Bomber Rothstein.*" It was feared that "*Bomber Rothstein has returned!*" And worst of all, that present anti-war movement troublemakers were now joined by old-guard Bolsheviks who loved blowing things up for their nefarious purposes.

Though even as speculation this generated gray hairs on any law official, a saner, calmer reporter confirmed as of press time the elder Rothstein still "*. . . resided peacefully in Israel and had for over a decade as an honored guest of the Masad.*"

The basic message was not, however hypothetical: Their collective resumes gave Student a good long pause. His long-standing policy of keeping his nose clean, law-wise, included not being blown to smithereens, nor ending up in irons for colluding with those who did.

In the next few days, Milly — infuriated at the *Examiner* and *Chronicle* — made sure Student heard the truth about her father, Samuel Rothstein. She emphasized the capitalist presses policy was to smear people of the old time radical left.

"Student, there is so much *mythology* about Daddy. He is a very gentle man. He wept when our pet bird died."

The Guild artistic committee — or those not incarcerated beyond questioning — met at Big Lena's All Star Café for a follow up. Milly maintained steely resolve about the need for a socialist drama, only strengthened by the night before.

In view of the increased oppression of the government, Milly suggested the opening night performance of *The Lower Depths* be May first, and a charity presentation be given on *Cinco de Mayo*.

Simon Conners — despite his admiration for Milly and her pedigree — was far more practical about this multi-cultural gesture.

"Milly, I don't know if Gorky and a bunch of socialist Mexicans on May fifth would be a good mix. May first though, it *is* a good idea."

Student announced he would miss the next meeting. He must go to Iowa for Christmas, for he had not seen his parents in over fifteen months.

A casting call for *Depths* would be set sometime in early January, and Student's recently completed course in theater would be put to severe test. Prior to his departure, this term project was to direct a Christmas children's play at a large Episcopalian church. This was baptism by fire.

Mother of God, weren't there enough issues in this new academic path of his?

This part of his theater practicum was more daunting (for

him) than a first time jump for a sky diver. Student's only chance for success was using the teachers as buffers between him and the kids.

Didn't a director of a drama have enough to do without fretting about his lead peeing his pants, or the villain being asleep in the set when the curtain went up?

During his previous times at school he was not social and tended to a fondness of books and movies. Children he considered part of his future wife's concern. When planning the *World Together*, he was grateful Debbie did all the dreaming in the children sector. And because of this lack of contact with children, he became averse to them in any setting and assumed he had no affinity for bouncy-bouncy on the knee, and playing patty-cake with the wee ones.

Furthermore — perhaps more than anything — Student suspected this discreet phobia was aggravated by the raucous, semi-domesticated brood his sister and her *Husband the Dentist* hatched in whatever tree they nested. Loath to farm living, she had fled rural Iowa early, mating in a far distant Iowa county. This exposure to children gave Student incipient heebie-jeebies, perhaps the root cause to these qualms about his theater practicum.

In a major revelation, Student discovered his fear of children disappeared during the process leading up to the Saturday-Sunday performances of *Aaron and the Good Shepherd*. It was replaced by an interest and admiration in people, like him, who once were so young.

There was a revealing charm in experiencing minds yet unimpeded by setbacks like forgetting your line, where to stand or forgetting to put on your left shoe. Such mishaps would destroy an adult.

But thanks to the Gods who blessed the legendary Thespis,

it went remarkably well — with six curtain calls and two dozen yellow roses — but most generously a box of *Milk Duds* for each cast member.

Student found himself strangely proud — this directing business was catchy. Something stirred inside and it felt more positive than anything he'd experienced before.

8.

He sat in his father's hatchery listening to him espouse producing the perfect chicken on a completely self-sustaining chicken farm: This concept was defined by the patriarch as having "Zip comes down the road, but a fully plump chicken going out to market, and of course the perfect egg."

It was his father's quest — his dream, the legendary *Self-Sustaining Chicken Farm*. But since Student's first memory, his Dad's quest was always — cruelly — thwarted by an onslaught of diverse natural evils.

"But now I'm close, Student. Right on top of it, as it were."

The two drank coffee in the only place certainly protected against his sister's four children and her *Husband the Dentist* — there to make a screaming muddle out of Christmas. It was tragic enough that attendance was mandatory during Christmas dinner. Both father and son would have gladly hired proxies for the task. However there was no such thing for Christmas dinners, and this ordeal was just ahead of them.

Upon the hatchery door a sign read, *"No Entry: Eggs-A-Pipping"* His dad kept coffee maker and such in here, and his vast library on poultry and allied topics.

His father could tolerate the grandchildren and his sister's constant yakking, but her *Husband the Dentist* overwhelmed even the gracious heart of his father. The fool professed himself a businessman. He was dedicated to advising his father-in-law how to join the real business world, and move his chicken business whole cloth onto the main track of American Industry and beyond.

"After all," *Husband the Dentist* would say, ". . . the real money these days is in high productivity first and acceptable quality second. Chickens are not a connoisseur commodity, Dad."

Student, or worse, his Aunt Lila, sometimes argued with the dolt.

How could an avaricious tooth puller possibly understand his father's vision? The two's concepts of quality were far apart — further than the foreign policies of the Soviet Union and Monaco.

Pouring his Dad a cup of his own shepherd's brew coffee Student sounded him out on a family rumor.

"Aunt Lila said you agreed with Mom to retire to Florida once you had two or more years of the perfect chicken farm. And I'm really for it. You're sixty six and Mom only a few years younger."

His father toyed with his mother's gift, a tiny tool kit 'with a thousand uses,' perfect for him. He aimed a keen eye on his son,

"Partially true. I did. But my promise did not assure Florida. Anyway, once I have two years of perfection, just to prove to the doubters, I will honorably retire to warmer climes to write a book about it all."

Then, he was sure, his discovery would spread worldwide.

Student realized — in a second epiphany — that his father was as possessed by his inspiration and ideology as the various labor activists at the BTWG were about theirs. But his father was possessed by gentler forces who—with his mother's help — protected him.

His father looked up at this best friend and son — there was little time left between them and the ordeal of Christmas dinner,

"Debbie's father feels lousy about what Debbie pulled on you: You out serving your country and his daughter is doing the opposite, is his view. Very patriotic guy. He asks after you, Student. He was really looking forward to having you as a son-in-law."

Did his father feel responsible to say this? Was he sounding out Student on Debbie? Student experienced a shot of anger but kept silent on the matter.

Actually, neither his parents nor he had any use for Debbie's religiously overboard father. His mother's policy was more forthcoming on creatures like Debbie's father.

"It goes against the Lord's wisdom that such a bully fathered a beautiful and kindly person like Deborah. And the poor mother spends her time holding her peace and reading the Bible."

A comfortable silence soothed both father and son. He reached over and put a hand on Student's shoulder — his father was not without a sense of humor. There was more than just one challenge ahead for this Christmas dinner.

"You know, your Aunt Lila is bringing her present steady. God help that son-in-law of mine if he says anything mutton-headed. My little sister is a force of nature."

Student — other than see his father and mother — took joy seeing Aunt Lila, the Notorious Lady of Kossuth County, Iowa. She had her own 25 acre place, was a librarian for the school district and drove the county Bookmobile. She remained indubitably and proudly single despite great beauty retained into her present day sixties.

Pursuits of her by all Kossuth County swains were forever frustrated — and she would date a younger man just as readily as an older. Worse, it was known that she occasionally hosted men overnight.

That *did it* for sniffier county residents.

Some of these unsuccessful swains, with savagely pent-up sexual desires, had attained positions of local influence and sought revenge. They launched drives to fire her on morality charges.

Those miserable half-wits were at once outflanked by Aunt Lila — like Napoleon at Austerlitz. After a few times, no one ever tried again.

On Christmas Eve he drove over to the county bus farm where she was working on the bookmobile. Unable to hug him because of coveralls spotted with grease, she simply leaned forward and delivered an expert peck to his lips.

"You haven't fathered any children out in San Francisco yet, have you Student?"

While he rolled his eyes theatrically at such an idea she read a quick passage in the service manual then dabbed away a bit of grease from her cheek with a rag.

"And Debbie? Do you harbor hard feelings towards her?"

"And why shouldn't I? Our plans are shot. Whoopee meant more to her than I, that's clear."

"Student, don't be harsh on Debbie. In the last few years, this love and sex stuff went epidemic. Certainly you have discovered that by this time."

He let the matter drop and Lila did also. Instead they concentrated resources on backing the bookmobile from the barn. The hapless vehicle was close to its end; it squatted forlornly on its frame; the suspension long gone.

"Aunt Lila, great Scott! It's too old — too many books."

"Nonsense. Can't have too many books aboard the old girl."

She ducked into the rear corridor, cramming feet into snow boots, popping out of the coveralls and reappearing as the librarian. Christmas Eve or no, she had a presentation. Lila returned to the driver's seat, hopping on one foot to secure a recalcitrant left boot.

"Our ordeal is tomorrow with that popinjay of a brother-in-law of yours. If my big brother won't defend himself I will."

She then shrugged into her winter coat; both looked out the windshield at the drab scene. Wind blew ribbons of snow along its featureless path. Winter had closed its icy fist around the entire land.

"Miss Iowa winters?"

"No."

They moved to Student's car, shrugging into the blast of air from the car's heater. While underway towards the presentation, she looked at her nephew, voice assuming a serious, even instructional tone, a rarity between them.

"Be respectful, Student. Women are half of the world's population."

On the red-eye back to San Francisco her words stood out from the lively St. Nick's day debate between Aunt Lila and *Husband the Dentist*. He mulled them over as the craft sped westward.

The initial casting call was a dud. Only a half dozen people showed. Three of them had acted in *Depths* on its disastrous first night in 1958, Freddy O'Malley and two others. Milly had been the set designer, as she would again — this time with an ample budget.

So those four who had not acted in *Depths*, or in fact at all, did readings and went home disappointed with only the traditional "We'll call you," to ease their discomfort.

"Why didn't you just sign them on board, Student?"

Davy Boy — who to Student's dismay was the guild's Sergeant At Arms — supported the concept that belief-in-social-message equaled ability. Student mulled over the setback while Milly explained to Davy Boy that the level of ability regards casting was the only criteria a good theater director used. Then, they launched into a *"YAID,"* (**Y**et **A**nother **I**deological **D**iscussion), time-consuming flaws in any gathering of the BTWG. Student simply closed the matter — a Director did casting, and he knew that.

"I am going to put out a casting call to all the colleges, and indeed any place with actors interested in pursuing the stage. We either put it on with the seriousness that the creator intended, or not at all."

Milly, Davy Boy, Freddy O'Malley, and Simon Conners looked at Student as if he'd sprouted antlers; always the quiet bystander, this was his first dictum as *Herr Direktor.*

 Had he not won his spurs maneuvering, wheedling, and cajoling 7-10 year old's around, plus their teachers and not a few parents? He was ready for the BTWG. O'Malley didn't like this at all, and gestured outside.

"We'll end up with all sorts involved. They won't give a big flying fuck about what Gorky and the entire socialist experience is about."

O'Malley looked indignantly to others for reaffirmation. The President Emeritus put his unlit pipe into his mouth, puffed absently a couple of hits, and then shrugged.

"Does an actor have to believe in the message of the play?"

Davy Boy, more a movie fiend than the theater squinted — putting his recollective faculties a whirling.

"Well, Lillian Gish was a real cunt and she played kindly old grandmothers."

"Davy Boy! Shame on you."

Milly would have none of that nonsense.

Seeing his ship was veering off course, Student patted his hand on the table for order. Time to apply his recent navy experience: It was a matter of assigning a sailor to a detail they were keen to avoid.

"A director's most vital responsibility is casting, and there are many actors who are looking for experience."

Milly looked at him with a blink, for Student right before her and the others had become The Man with the Plan. Her look turned to one of admiration.

Student felt like a butterfly sporting a snazzy new set of wings.

"Well, then that's it. I'm buying coffee."

And Simon Conners rose, took a fresh lungful of air, and nodded with satisfaction: Fact was, they didn't have a green-as-the-hills director, but one foolish enough to take charge. In the end, it would all be Student's fault.

Student wondered if it was pure hormones that activated his primordial urges stirring with asp-like slithering: Knowing that O'Malley was soon to start a post-holiday sentence of 14 days for contempt of court, he saw possibilities.

He wondered if during his absence Milly might want to lower the petty bourgeois barrier that impedes creativity between the genders? Would this not be even more crucial to the debut of *Depths* going on May first, International Workers Day?

While ascending to his aerie on the 3rd floor of the hotel, he reflected the most professional way to start would be to read Gorky's play instead of scanning a crib. He followed the grim stairs to the 2nd floor, was about to make the turn to ascend to the third when he heard weeping — female weeping.

He stopped — listened, and knew it came from the hotel office, the upper half of the door open. Easing past the mailboxes, trying not to betray his presence by stepping too heavily on the maimed floorboards, he peeked into the apartment to see that the weeping came from Mrs. Smith. She sat in her chair before the television facing almost the opposite way of the door. This weeping was uncharacteristic for the sturdy woman. Eddy's position had a better view of the door, but he usually didn't care.

Student moved carefully into view Hawkeye-style.

Between her and Eddy sat a large paper bag with a bottleneck protruding. From the looks of both Smiths it was either empty or close to it. Though not unusual for Mrs. Smith to imbibe with Eddy they were normally a chatty amiable pair. Something had gone wrong.

"You rotten bastard. I treat you like my Prince Charming and you talk to me like shit. Say awful things. "

She put a handkerchief up to her nose, gave it a swipe, and then allowed a modest ends-up hit from the bagged container.

"That's right; keep your damned mouth shut now. It's too late. See what you made of me? I'm drinking right from the bottle like a whore. So, damage is done."

Pity for the mawkish pair was absent from Student's busy soul, and he was about to turn and sneak off when something stopped him. He peeked back in at the conflicted couple.

Though Eddy was a stoic soul, he seemed to have attained new heights. He didn't even bat an eye at her name-calling. But, the most compelling clue that something was terribly wrong flickered away on the television. Playing was a soap opera, and Eddy never watched anything that didn't have *Manhood* stamped on it; lacking this, he would leave it run and read a racing form or simply fall asleep.

Instead he watched a soap opera keenly. Or doggedly? Student was so perplexed he stepped fully into the doorway, and the thoroughly soused Mrs. Smith still did not see him.

"I bet you didn't call your wife a whore."

She lifted the bottle, tried a fruitless hit from the spent

vessel, and then put it down allowing a disgusted grunt.

"Plus you drank all the VO. I buy good stuff, and you sop it up like a dry sponge." She swung and slapped his arm. "Next time you buy the likker."

She fished around in her capacious bosom for her pack of cigarettes, found none. Student noticed that the impact of her none-too-gentle backhand caused its recipient's head to move slightly left — away from the TV. Also, the impact of her slap left a dent, as if her backhand were delivered to a sack of sand.

Eddy was dead.

Student reached, tripped the inside handle and entered. This was a situation no one prepared him for. He looked over Eddy carefully, determining that indeed the fellow was dead,

"Professor, you should knock before coming in."

Mrs. Smith objected in the mildest tones; Student conveyed as gently as possible the dark news, "Mrs. Smith, I'm awfully sorry to tell you this, but Eddy has passed away."

She turned, looked at her companion — then back up at Student, shook her head and added wonderingly,

"Jesus! The hell you say?"

And fell asleep at once, her head falling to her bosom emitting a consoling snore.

Student lay on his bed an hour later. He replayed events, including the first responders — a set of uniformed cops. When they saw Mrs. Smith and Eddy they fretted there were two dead people not the one reported. Student quickly corrected,

"No, Mrs. Smith is asleep."

The older of the two took up his Billy club and moved Eddy around carefully, shrugged and put the club away.

"No bullet holes, stab wounds — doesn't look like he was

strangled."

His partner looked into the paper bag removed the bottle and shook his head,

"Naw, drank himself to death, poor bastard. Too high grade a booze."

They made a phone call, sat and waited the arrival of the morgue wagon. Student thought there would be questions; they had none, their curiosities long absent.

Student returned to his room, and thoughts of Gorky's play, the BTWG, and issues about other things receded. He sat heavily on his bed, hearing its springs complain of great age. Fully clothed, he stretched out and looked at the ceiling; yellowed, narrow streaks of tobacco stains extended towards the walls. In a bizarre mind-flow, Student watched these stains waif about in abstract renditions of *A plus B Hotel* death spirits.

An ironic truth came to him: Despite his years — now almost 30 on this crowded planet — including his military service, some of it taking him to a war zone, Eddy's was the first corpse he had ever seen.

Certainly this could not be true, and he reviewed memories with an earnest recollective sweep — but nothing. Eddy's demise from premium whiskey was it.

He closed his eyes to concentrate.

Opening them, the light seemed to have shifted in the room. Had he dozed off? Student's mind whirled: Finding a dead man watching television while being scolded by his partner —too stupefied with liquor to realize he was dead — sent Student sliding even further down the incline from societal normalcy.

Likewise, the comfortable middle path of American fulfillment was also drifting further away.

A knock on his door gave pause. When he asked who it was they just came in — not locking his door was a mortal sin in the world of the *A plus B Hotel,* and he had committed it.

"We're from the Federal Bureau of Investigation. You are Student Patterson?"

For the second time today, he was looking at an F.B.I. badge and I.D. The first, had been at the college alongside a defensive, sardonic Jenkins who took the lead in responding.

The feds had thus far been unsuccessful in locating both the party who planted the bomb in their car, or the organization behind it. The F.B.I.s hounds were everywhere looking for any shred of evidence. They had only managed to provoke O'Malley to insult the Federal Magistrate but had nothing more on him.

"We would like to ask you a few follow ups, Mr. Patterson."

One asked away — innocuous, even arcane stuff — while the other scanned his room with hungry eyes coming to rest on his officer's sword — the only wall decoration of his otherwise dismal room. He pointed to it when his partner paused for oxygen.

"I was an enlisted man, so no sword. Pretty snazzy," and he looked at Student who had risen to a sitting position. ". . . mind?"

"No, go ahead. It was the cheapest I could buy, but it is real enough."

While the agent removed it, looking it over his partner finally launched a question of undisguised guile.

"Does Mr. O'Keefe know you had sexual relations with Miss Rothstein? He's a violent man, Mr. Patterson."

The other agent took sword out of its sheath a few inches, then clicked it back, adding,

"Yup. Might need this sword — O'Malley is all of six-four, weighs in maybe 250 pounds. When he was inside, he picked up a prison guard and stuffed him in a laundry cart. The gorilla got an extra six months for that."

"Mr. O'Malley is the lead in my play, and we have a good relationship."

"But you did not answer my question."

"Gentlemen don't answer such questions."

Both agents glanced at each other swapping Cheshire smiles; hanging the sword back up the agent stepped back, running an admiring finger along the sheath.

"Genuine enough. Still, you might need it."

Student shifted his attentions to his inane sword, and found voice and motive for what both the bastards deserved,

"I have already needed it, as you say. Because of the French influence in Southeast Asia, the North Vietnamese were especially fearful of a razor sharp sword, more so than firearms, oddly."

"Really?"

"Though my Form 151 says I was aboard ship for a year, you guys have clearances so I can tell you: I was on two separate covert operations upriver with a Navy gun boat. And in the villages, you go down a line of men and shoot them one at a time, they would never inform. But," and here Student stood, took the sword off the wall and held it out, ". . . you line a half dozen of them up, and slit their throats one by one, by the time you get to the third or fourth one, they would tell the translator everything we came there to get and more. Odd isn't it — it was this sword. I found out quite by accident — lost my cool and just did-in one for the meanness of it. Hated the little swine."

Both agents took a long look at him then the sword. Student drew it out halfway, then slid it back.

"You get blood stains off with a mixture of bicarbonate of soda and lemon juice. Nothing else works. "

He looked down fondly at his weapon — as a pet owner

might a spaniel or cat just groomed. The agents finished with a few cursory items, left their card on the table and vanished — wisps of steam. He guessed they wouldn't be back.

Student felt badly about Milly: Evidently as the daughter of the legendary Bomber Rothstein the feds felt obliged to follow her. He did not need a second government encounter concerning his sex life — the first was a military infraction, and now this.

If he told her then what might be the point? The more immediate point was that the FBI could use such a smear to provoke O'Malley into throttling Student, or some such felonious assault. This would put the Dunsmuir Bomber behind bars for several years — if not more. They had tried everything to pin that night's bombing on O'Malley, but nothing worked.

They even ran Davy Boy through the mill, but he took occasion to preach socialist doctrine to the unwashed. And Milly? She had not mentioned them questioning her. She was now with O'Malley, and together they certainly could care for themselves when it came to the Feds.

There might be an appearance of Student acting in his own interests, but he was sure that was untrue. The wisest route was to get on with casting the play — for the play was the thing; everyone since Aeschylus knew that.

9.

Seers of Future Present

(Elder Men and Women dressed as Chinese New Year's celebrants)

Student, many warnings were given you since Debbie tossed you over for a big hippie from New York. But you have made nothing of our warnings. Now approaches the true, hardest test of your humanity. The issue is — will you be equal to learning anything from the morass you have so wrongheadedly leaped into?

Despite our gifts as seers, we cannot predict the outcome with accuracy because you have been consistently such a heedless dumb bunny. Can't you see how you have affronted the ancient female forces?! They are so disgusted with you they deny us fair hearing.

Take heed: Your personal Armageddon approaches; you will be humiliated and so disgrace your good family name; they'll probably kick you out of that sleazy hotel as morally unfit. But even in the face of this, we are on your side and will be supplicants in your interests, In the event you wonder what our motivation is, we are very dedicated and benevolent seers.

The invitation to Jenkins' academic shindig specified the first night of the Chinese New Year of the Rooster, 1969.

"Are you then required to dress up like a chicken?"

Student enjoyed his college office alone until the new quarter saw the empty desk occupied by a horse's ass named William Monkers.

In addition to his lame sense of humor, he was stupid enough to adopt Milton as his thesis topic. Student did his best to encourage him.

"Milton is as interesting as baby poop."

"Oh, that is unfortunate disparagement for someone in the discipline."

Monkers protested by removing his new pipe from his mouth, and jabbing it nowhere in particular. He had all the Hugh Hefner gestures down pat, along with a working knowledge of the famous theologian's "The Playboy Philosophy." Student's unlikely high-profile invitation to this bash-for-the-influential prompted his levity but was a cover for verdant envy.

Monkers normally sat with his face hanging into public space — yet seeing the garish rooster lithograph with red border on the invitation — now famous college-wide — he squirmed close and draped his face over Student's shoulder.

Student put the invitation back in the envelope, handed it to him over his shoulder and said,

"Here you can have it. Just say you're me. Chinese New Year is not on my church calendar."

It was pushed right back, and even Monkers couldn't conceal his shock.

"What in hell is wrong with you, Student! Don't you realize that every tenured faculty person in the University is vying for an invitation to that celebration! Jenkins is married to the Chairman of the Board of Regents, you're not tenured, nor even faculty, you lucky bastard."

Dear God, but I've had it with this ass, lamented Student and began abandon ship procedures: He scraped enough notes and *Lower Depth* script copies together for the casting call tonight at the BTWG, stuffed them in his swelled case along with the invitation and escaped. He fast-walked the three blocks to the pizza parlor where he could think, or perhaps not think. Either was OK.

He sniffed in familiar pizza aroma while concealed in the semi-shadows. He was immeasurably more comfortable even here — at the site of the now legendary mayhem following a discharged firearm. Student's part was forgiven but would never be forgotten, especially by the owner.

With this quiet, he would think this invitation business through.

Student would need to be deaf and unsighted to be unaware of the convocation of upcoming swells at the Jenkins estate on Chinese New Year. His invitation was the only surprise albeit a lousy one.

All college gossip masticated away tirelessly on Jenkins' college situation. Years before, the misanthropic soul made an uncharacteristically advantageous marriage: Mrs. Jenkins was wealthy, the daughter and great granddaughter of two former California Governors, and related through diverse lineages to three former U.S. Senators and a gaggle of Congressmen from a half-dozen California districts populated by those with money, influence and lots of time.

But that was not all. Her purest blood connection was through her great-great-great grandfather who in 1815 hoodwinked resident Indians out of the entire San Francisco Peninsula with five crates of fabric, three axes and a moldy bale of burlap. This completed, he had out-of-work caballeros run them out, or if they were young enough — sold as slaves to coastal traders.

You couldn't have a purer claim as a Founding Father to California than that.

Envious individuals, even lofty academics who never took less than two hour lunches, would attend. But the finest grist for the gossip was how Mrs. Jenkins was many years older than her husband, and how Jenkins went about in absolute terror of her. *"If our naughty little boy steps out of line,"* Student heard one tenured Don tell another, " . . . *the old girl will throw his radical posterior from her money-laden Olympus."*

How accurate was this shop-talk? On his academic turf Jenkins was a force to be reckoned with. He had ready command of his discipline, and applied it ruthlessly if he were crossed. Lastly, he never missed a step right or left when it came to calling on his academic prerogatives.

In any case, Student wouldn't go to this social and academic whirly-gig. He didn't have dinner attire, nor would his newly purchased 1962 Dodge Dart be appropriate, for valet parking was stipulated. The previous owner had a bumper sticker on the Dart reading *"Eat my Zucchini,"* and Student could not scrape it away. He had purchased the dented machine way under market because of its arcane right-hand drive.

When served his pizza the owner put a small envelope under the tray.

"From your fearless leader — the prick."

What must he do for safe haven? Occupy his dismal room at the hotel full time?

He opened it, lamenting his discovery of another Jenkins gift, a quasi-mind reading ability, for the message was at least one step ahead.

"Don't worry about the dinner attire; a tie will do. If you

don't come, the entire grant will be jeopardized. I'm putting you up for display; they don't make them any more establishment than you. Good luck at casting. (Jenkins)."

Student drank his beer and bit away a hunk of pizza half-heartedly. He at once desired stronger spirits. The post-Eddy death at the hotel had kicked off a spiritual backsliding. Now he must act a role in a faux Sino-Euro masque. Student was miserable at any gathering reeking of lick-spittles and galloping egos.

But the hell with it! Tonight was his first *real* casting call as an independent director:

Shouldn't he be more optimistic about this? The casting call went out to all regional academic and community theaters. Both he and Milly received dozens of queries for directions to the arcane location of the Haywood Playhouse.

He was relieved to have Milly — a veteran player and stage person — for help. Milly's main man, Freddy O'Malley, was enjoying his last free night. Tomorrow morning U.S. Marshalls would escort him to a comfy two weeks behind bars for contempt of court.

O'Malley was generously spending his last free night trying out despite his casting being pro-forma. His theater instructors warned Student about directors making pro-forma casting. Yet as Milly and O'Malley said, he had acted in the play dozens of times plus stayed active in the prison drama club.

Student's first and absolute resolution was to avoid anything vaguely sexual with Milly. Though it occurred to him the FBI could be running a bluff, it was best to be on the safe side.

Morally, Student wanted to recover from his recent set-backs, especially his Bacchanal in Saigon. He reflected with remorse on his weakened moral state subsequent to his derailment from the American straight and narrow.

For twelve years between Junior High and graduate school — he rehearsed with Debbie dual roles as idealized husband and father. In this role he, and she, were content and unquestioning. The couple were confident of eventual reward. They would stride along a metaphorical state fair midway between kitchen appliances on the right and that year's new-model station wagons on the left.

Overhead, instead of a tramway, would be a walkway of polished hardwood where Astaire and Rogers impersonators tapped danced and swung — kicks, swirls and jumps. And song, certainly song; their lyrics would say it all for him and Deborah, *"Heaven, I'm in heaven."*

Made no difference now.

This cake walk of normalcy was shot to hell, left to sputter out in the muck. Would his end be similar to Eddy? What were the late Eddy's accomplishments prior to becoming a bump-on-the-log as Mrs. Smith's live-in and fellow intoxicant? Did he at one time —with his betrothed — have a promising future in post-war middle-of-the-roadism?

Student was now off the rails; he followed a headless horseman into a sordid world. The memory of strong drink rose within Student — a vaporous phantom promising relief. But — Mother of God, if this phantom were heeded, would it be the end of Student?

10.

When he arrived at the Butcher Town Writer's Guild the tryout line was around the corner. Davy Boy functioned at peak sobriety as Sergeant of Arms. He had the look of mission-intensity,

"Doors are locked until it is time, Student. I'll escort you in. I'm searching these characters for guns and shit."

Inside, the Thespian Committee was sitting in a jigsaw pose of stunned disbelief, save for Milly who was jubilant.

"Oh, Student. Isn't it wonderful. Your idea was brilliant. Just brilliant."

And it started there, extending to a long, long night — a great, pleasing contrast to the first casting call.

Actual tryouts took place in back of the drawn curtain on the new stage — at Student's insistence ('Privacy is needed for the artistic dignity of the process.') with Milly and O'Malley reading parts to the applicants. For the most part they were young, from diverse academic drama departments plus regional and community theaters.

Their group were a contemporary study in popular attire: Nehru shirts, bell bottoms, skinny pants, maxi and miniskirts, vests, sandals, flip flops, no shoes at all, sashes, head bands, head and facial hair in all lengths and design, then there was a smattering of robes, capes, mantles, caftans, saffron gowns, and one potential Thespian in buckskin which he/she deemed Native American garb.

A few out-of-step sorts wore sports clothes, and one even a suit and tie. Student felt sorry for the poor devil.

But they could have all worn togas (there were none of them, surprising enough) and Davy Boy liked none of it. He stayed constantly on the look-out for weapons. His office made him keen for interlopers.

"They're all unarmed, but sure as hell there are FBI infiltrators and John Birchers in with the other crazy bastards, so watch yourselves. I don't trust any of them."

Student reverted in a good way to his navy days when Officer of the Deck and responsible for the navigation of a 350 foot ship through stormy nights and days. Even calm weather bore responsibility with the assortment of malcontents and semi-criminals on the "Bugly" all skilled at negligence and malingering.

Milly's expertise was his lifeline, and she saved Student's posterior from embarrassments and screw ups. She contrasted with O'Malley who brusquely told unsuccessful candidates, *"Not everyone can be an actor."*

Student and Milly would compensate, trying to soothe these souls' spirits. Finally Student told O'Malley that he was hurting peoples' feelings. He became angry — exchanging unpleasant words with Milly who defended Student — and walked out. She explained his unpromising behavior,

"He really is a very sensitive man, but going to jail again, even for only a few days, has him on edge."

Federal and State officials were huffing and puffing down his rear, doing everything possible to pin the bomb planted in the FBI vehicle on O'Malley. Evidently, Student allowed, the unceasing pressure from this quarter was making him testy. As a director, he must start making allowances.

Just past midnight Student — work done — was spent. He was about to leave when Milly diffidently showed him sketches of her set design. They were superb; *Depths* was anything but easy as a visual to the audience. Characters were everywhere; staging had to allow the audience to see it all.

And all this within a believable setting — which was in effect, a turn of the century flophouse, Russian style.

"I went to school for set design. My mother insisted. She herself was quite an artist."

She left him to look at the drawings, hurrying off to spend O'Malley's last free night together. The BTWG President Emeritus Simon Conners startled him when he parted the curtain and entered.

Sitting, he loaded up his capacious pipe.

"Well, I was way off base thinking your casting method was wrong. I've got to admire you. Helluva night."

He took out a pint of wickedly fine Irish Whiskey from his coat pocket, produced two shot glasses from another. They drank to even more successes. He looked fondly at the set design, and recalled Milly's numerous talents and skills to get things done. His pipe going full snort, he blinked sadly looking at the rich threads of smoke rise into the works.

"O'Malley doesn't treat Millicent very well, the bastard, so of course she is devoted to him."

He poured another round, leaving that contradictory declaration hanging out there. Student admired Simon Conners — he talked little, never proselytized and seemed a saner representative of American socialism than he'd imagined. Actually he was similar to his father.

They sat enjoying a Celtic rush giving Student time to realize he was experiencing his first success in a long time. He didn't need to love *The Lower Depths* — not even to understand it absolutely. It was a play; his job was to present it to an audience in a coherent and attention-grabbing way.

His career in the transport of frozen sirloin steaks and ice cream had concluded; another became suddenly apparent.

He brought his homework to his hotel, now a place of anxiety for residents. Since Eddy's passing Mrs. Smith had lapsed into a boozy state of mourning. In her cups she lionized Eddy — how he had been the finest man she ever knew, *". . . and I've known a lot of them, Professor, as they say, I've done them all, the long, the short and the tall."*

Sober, the poor woman would sooner be caught naked than utter such gritty speech, but alcohol swept aside social graces. But ordinary life stumbled along: Most residents stayed in their rooms drunk or otherwise involved. Of course, there were always worries about fire, but in the event of such, Student's room was on the fire escape, a premium locale. So he slept with relatively few existential worries.

The following day was almost optimistic. Student was busy writing various notes and diverse preparations for the first rehearsal when there was a quiet knock on the door. He had cleverly installed a tiny mirror at the top of his transom in the event it was a drunk Mrs. Smith. Equally unwanted was his 'up corridor' neighbor who usually had an in-room dinner invitation for him and a head job as dessert.

A tiny edge of the caller was visible in the mirror; he saw it was Milly. She never visited his room before, and hopes raised.

He thought an admission to Milly of increasing bourgeois tensions would be beautiful timing. Perhaps Milly would help ease them.

She entered carrying an artist's portfolio, and Student almost closed the door on a young girl with pigtails carrying several books who followed. She wore thick glasses, was dark and extremely skinny; the Rothstein resemblance was all there. He assumed with dismay this was grandma's day to baby sit.

"This is my daughter Ruth, Student. Today is her thirteenth birthday. I'm taking her to the zoo — but first I wanted to drop these off. I really would like your input on them — for the second act."

While Milly put her portfolio on his table and struggled to unzip it, the young girl looked shyly at Student. He was having trouble reckoning arithmetic and human reproduction. The girl, sharp as a razor, guessed his confusion,

"I know. Everybody thinks mother is my grandmother."

Milly warned,

"Ruth don't presume to read an adult's thoughts. It isn't nice."

"I thought nothing of the sort, Ruth."

"Yes you did. My mother is ancient."

This spread the embarrassment evenly. Student had to deal with disappointment, confusion, surprise.

"Your mother is no such thing."

Milly took out drawings, looked towards him and shrugged,

"Ruth is visiting from Israel where her father lives. I planned her stay for when Mr. O'Malley was on his trip."

"He's in jail."

Ruth smiled, smug with her correction, and put the books on the end of his bed; large opal-dark eyes landed and locked on his sword.

"Oh, neat! A sword! That for the communist play?"

"Not *communist*, young lady!"

Milly was having trouble with her outspoken progeny and her mouth stopped in mid-protest when she too caught sight of sword. Student gestured — a tour director of his room.

"I was in the Navy, and officers have swords. Tradition."

"Oh, neat! Did you kill pirates and mutineers with it?"

This bourgeois bloodlust went too far for Mom: There was

a less-than-gentle- exchange in Hebrew between them; Ruth sighed and opened her book and feigned deep reading. Student for no specific reason assumed Millicent's Jewishness was long behind her.

"You speak Hebrew, Milly?'

"Yes. Since I was a child. Not well. "

"No. Not well."

Ruth agreed without breaking stride. Milly braced herself with a good heavy inhalation, took out notes, seemed on the verge of explaining them, but asked,

"Student, can you drive very well? I know you drive."

"Yes."

"Well, her father provided a chauffeur driven car, and I won't allow that — and he knows that. But he is so paranoid from his work. So, I'm driving, but it is too huge."

"Mom is a *menace*. But it's bullet and bomb proof. That is *so* cool."

"You want me to drive you out to the zoo?"

"I'm sorry. But one of the conditions of her visit, is I don't convey Ruth on public transport."

And it was this series of unlikely events that led Student to driving a modified tank sans turret from downtown San Francisco to the zoo. He brought along his mail and a script for purposes of frequent waits. He owed Milly, and disappointment or no, he wanted to help. He should help.

While Milly and daughter watched the big cats devour hunks of elderly dead horses, Student sought out a place to read his mail. He found shelter at a table decorated with pigeon poop, the guilty parties were close by strutting around waiting for handouts.

It was Iowa Day in the mails. One from his mother, a second

from his father and then very refreshingly, his Aunt Lila — this would have all good local stuff in it.

His mother's news was the usual: His father was too old to be questing after the Holy Grail of the self-sustaining chicken farm in Iowa winters. But he maintained this holy relic was just around the corner. Then, at 38, Student's fecund sister was pregnant with yet another.

"Couldn't she at least have imagination enough to have an affair," Student muttered at the letter.

His father's missive was more agricultural:

He allowed leak the fact that his golden fleece was at hand! Student was just feeling cheer for them, when the final paragraph took a major leap off the leaf of paper and smacked him between the eyes.

"Debbie returned to the family place for the holidays and stayed. So I guess that means she got her teacher's certificate at Wisconsin."

Student slid the letters into his pocket. He surmised the contents and the reason for Aunt Lila's letter was related to this dismal news. Debbie, except for brief visits, had told Student numerous time she no more wanted to return home than she would a jail cell. Her father's rules, she had aired with relief, were history.

His father's news item meant trouble — he knew it.

He went to Aunt Lila's letter with serious apprehension, and indeed it held no mood changer: She got right down to it — Aunt Lila didn't drive the county bookmobile for nothing. It was a moving 12 wheel tabloid. If it happened in the county, she knew about it.

Debbie is living back home and is pregnant. She came to the bookmobile, and is at least six months along. No husband or father is apparent. There is much dismay at her home. To her father, we are still in the Coolidge Administration here in Kossuth County, Iowa. So, despite her parents' wealth and prominence (especially her father) Debbie won't ever get work teaching full time or as a substitute. I know your father, and he would have told you she is back, but since he hides from reality on his idealized chicken farm, he will know little and deny even more. Student now listen to your Aunt Lila; Debbie is no longer that naive young Betty Crocker wannabe. She will soon give birth, and all her goal posts will change radically. I alert you to this with full knowledge you have your own life out there, and have moved on for the better. (Love, Lila)

"Bad news, Student?"

He returned from Iowa back to the Zoo — or at least this zoo. He faced Milly who was holding a bag of diverse purchases and rubbing a foot. He hastened to put the letter away.

"From Iowa. It is indeed bad news." He experienced a ribbon of selfishness. "But not for me. Where is Ruth?"

"She has a friend explaining the life history of the hippopotamus to her." She gestured to where Ruth stood before an outside grotto listening to a young man lecturing, gestures and all.

Was it a surprise that he cared far less for the news concerning Debbie than Aunt Lila anticipated? Debbie advocated free living so now was riding the train she so assertively wanted. Student's destination had diverged from hers and he had his own considerable problems. He had the damned Chinese New Year's gathering before him — in less than 48 hours he would be carrying the banner of the BTWG drama project before the monied elite.

"I'm guessing you are nervous about attending Professor Jenkins' New Year's celebration. You do look disconcerted."

"Somewhat, yes."

She finished rubbing one of the longest narrowest female feet he had ever seen, and shoved her shoe back on. 'Just how in hell old are you Milly?' was a pressing question, but of course a gentleman does not ask such. It was peculiar that Student wondered about her age now and not when they were having sexual encounters.

Certainly it was the appearance of this child — young child. That had to be it.

"None of us at the Guild could represent us like you will Student. Errol Strong will be there, and he is the *Examiner's* Wandering Critic, of course. A review by him would really, really be so unbelievable."

"I'll wear my officer's uniform, including sword. That'll do it."

She was such a serious woman — she looked hard at him, 'screwed up her eyes' as the Russian translators put it, before realizing that all wasn't right.

"You are kidding, Student. You would never do that."

"No, I would never do that."

No, he had steeled himself to labor through it all and scrape up formal wear, including a tie. However, this fantastic Chinese shindig became more daunting as every hour passed.

Returning from the zoo Student continued wondering why they used an armored transport for a thirteen year old girl. Also the FBI was following them, the two agents in the large sedan filled the front seat, like a pair of lowland gorillas. Student regretted his fabrication concerning his sword. Even at a distance, these two agents appeared capable of taking his sword and bending it around his neck.

"Do you know that the FBI is following you, Milly?"

Ruth beat her mother to the response.

"That's Abe and Arras from the consulate, Mr. Patterson. They protect me; that is so cool. They would make kasha out of the F.B.I. guys."

For the second time, Milly broke into Hebrew — a scolding Hebrew. The two vehicles stopped before the *A plus B Hotel*, a strange setting for possibly fifty thousand dollars of machinery.

"Her father, well, his job is what he always wanted. So he requires it, and you, young lady, take unseemly pride in it — being *served* by people" — she drew a breath and allowed an exasperated sigh — "people in a state of social equality should not serve one another."

"Why do you get so angry, Mother? I mean, Arras is such a great looking guy."

Student and Milly got out, and while heading towards the hotel entrance, Milly stopped Student by taking him gently by the shoulder and kissing him.

"Thank you Student, and good luck. I know you will do well; I just know."

While passing by the office, he peeked in, and was thankful to see Mrs. Smith alive but intoxicated in her chair staring at the television. She looked up and raised her hand in greeting.

"Professor, you're a real gentleman."

He thanked her and proceeded up the stairs. She was escorting in the Year of the Rooster with her own private ceremony.

11.

Seers of Future Present

(Men and Women Elders dressed in formal dinner wear)

Student, we warned you about the future, but you poor desolate man you just go forward, heedless, drawn to your nadir like Daedalus his forlorn heights. We remind you that however singular a horse's patoot you make out of yourself — no matter what happens — we are waiting to catch the pieces and reassemble your humanity. We will watch over you at all times, but even the Gods themselves at this point will not intercede. The dreaded Furies now rule and these ancients — feminism's eternal flames — despise you.

Student had four hours until the Chinese New Year circle sniff for the monied and prominent.

The day before began by solving problems logically. First he scraped together rented dinner attire, save for shoes and socks. These clothes even came with an instruction booklet informing the uninitiated in the ways and parlances of formal gatherings. ("Always be alert for specks of food on your clothing")

But now a second problem confronted, and it was formidable indeed.

The mishap began with innocent intentions. He would take

advantage of the BTWG's recent addition and benefit from the grant — a new pay phone.

He called Aunt Lila first, she could always be relied on for a fresh view of things, and she did not disappoint. Letting himself in the guild hall during the wee hours for maximum privacy he took out a roll of quarters and began.

Her phone was answered with a melodic "Miss Patterson's residence." He recognized that voice as he might his parents. It was Debbie. With light-speed reaction he hung up, putting the new phone through its first stress test. He was pole-axed by this implausible development.

Fumbling with more quarters he called his parents and when his mother answered he foolishly identified himself, even stuttering a bit.

"Yes Student. And this is your mother. I know it is you. It is wonderful to hear your voice."

And she laughed until he managed, "Mother, what in the world is Debbie doing at Aunt Lila's at 8:00 a.m. on a Sunday morning?"

It was her turn to stammer. He heard his father in the background, then her hand clapped over the receiver, then came off.

"Student, you had best talk to your father."

He knew the issue was a hard grounder between first and second, sending his home team scrambling for position. She listened to his father say something in the distance, then exasperated she continued, ". . . your father is going out to the extension in his shop, and Lord have mercy. We'll *both* talk."

"Give me a preview."

And it began: At first his mother, haltingly, then his father haltingly — for it was a no-nonsense halting development. Alternately, they explained Debbie either left or was ejected from her parent's home in the wake of an ugly fight.

What caused the kettle to boil over was her father. He was a tablet-totting bearded guardian of the Presbyterian ethic and had descended from the mount and spoken. He had the money to back up his plan.

He prepared and paid for all the legal and medical expenses for a see-no-baby adoption in Chicago, a lustful city if there ever was one. Debbie would then come home, recuperate, and then slink a thousand miles east to her Aunt's and start life over.

When Debbie found out the stork and its bundle were to be kicked out on its tail feathers, child and all, she refused, in disbelief he would even try such a thing.

In the ensuing maelstrom, she fled in bedroom slippers and walked the eight miles to Lila's, arriving barefoot. She took Debbie in indefinitely without reservation. To add her own ingredient to the brew, Lila called Debbie's father and offered cool appraisal of his humanity, breaking her phone when she hung up.

And the absolute confirmation that Student's enemy had indubitably entered his camp via a lowered gate, was his mother who added quietly — and without an iota of halting,

"And if Lila hadn't of, I would have," his father following with, "*We* would have."

His parents quickly explained that they of course loved Student forever. But despite their breakup, they had known Debbie since she was a kid, and loved her, and thought her father was cruel and hateful.

Student did a poor imitation of ending the conversation on a general, neutral basis with sort of a recap of today's news. After hanging up, he laid his forehead against a table where thousands of revolutionary conversations had taken place in over a half century.

Forming his right hand into a fist, he thumped the table softly, but increased intensity until it was quite loud.

"Mother of God! The enemy broached the ramparts!"

Student was the lead actor in his own morality play.

He still had over four hours and the Jenkins palace was less than 35 miles off. Student knew beyond all, he would never survive this ordeal without gentle anesthetizing, though he must be cautious not to overdo. With this new load on his mind, in addition to matters about the play, he needed assertive measures to find center. His mind needed ready wit to deal with this herd of stuffed shirts.

He bought a fifth of fine cognac, always his favorite. While struggling to make it fit into the Dart's glove compartment, he opened the bottle and took a nip. It was definitely appropriate stuff. Since it was in the right direction, Student stopped by Fort Winfield Scott and parked near the exact locale where Kim Novak's movie double took her leap into the sea in Hitchcock's *Vertigo*.

Debbie had the precise measurements of Kim Novak.

Now, why on earth had he thought of that?

He popped open the glove compartment, sneaked a look left and right, took out the cognac and allowed a heavy hit.

It cost a mint but went down like honey except it was smoother. Also, unlike the stuff of bees, it took immediate medicinal action.

Why in the name of all that was rational had he made the phone calls to Iowa twelve hours before? And the day before this awful New Year's business. He had a notion to punch the Dodge Dart into gear and follow Novak's double.

But then again what was so illogical about such phone calls?

He made many home before. Must he fear the enemy everywhere in this ant hill of a world?

He went to replace the cognac in the glove compartment, thought better and bumped the last hit with another — this one a tad more modest.

Any frustration with his family's blue-plate treatment of Debbie was mitigated significantly by Student keeping the home folk ignorant about the precise words in Debbie's letter dismissing Student from her life — especially the part about him murdering Asian children. Would they so adore her if they knew about her ghastly accusation?

And he saw no reason to tell his family about her harebrained and mawkish statement about sex. This latter part of her missive contrasted harshly with her current plight. Debbie now gestated kick-ass proof she didn't know what in hell she was writing about.

He still held the cognac, remembered its place in the glove compartment and before replacing it allowed another small hit on this Debbie business and repeated out loud what could become a mantra.

Well, Iowa is Iowa, and that is their problem. I have mine.

He consulted the map Milly drew and thought of a positive. Had not this news about Debbie's disgrace provide him increased strength-of-resolve for the evening's task? He was aboard a sort of ship and knew well the course ahead, every degree and minute of it.

Student's native abilities at navigation made it obvious that he didn't need a map. He turned off the highway, climbed into the Marin County Hills — giants to anyone from Iowa — and followed his instincts. The Dart huffed its doughty way up, a brave craft.

He was looking for a 70 acre estate, with a quarter mile long driveway lined with 100 Norfolk Island Pines. *"It is very singular; we've protested there several times,"* Milly told him *". . . it is worth more than the food budget for a third world city, and they manage to pay no taxes at all."*

Most impressive to Student was this tax-free manor sat on a promontory overlooking the sweep of the open Pacific. So what if its deadbeat tax responsibility could feed all of Brazil or Argentina? He respected Milly but was no socialist. He kept silent at the BTWG, but Student felt Milly and others were clinging to dinosaur skeletons sliding into the tar pits.

A great colossus of money sucking down everyone into the blackest of hells, he thought, immediately admiring this astute social observation.

When he came within sight of the ocean he pulled the Dart over and gazed out upon his old ally, the Pacific Ocean, blue and endlessly wise. To celebrate visiting his old friend he allowed himself another hit of cognac, checked the time, and saw he was early. It was still light, a glowing red and gold on the western horizon.

Student reviewed his plan — actually, arrived at one:

He would slip in at eight, locate Jenkins before his chairman got mentally blotto. Student would do the minimum amount of schmoozing, then get the hell out of there and head home. He was confident that during that brief time, he could radiate all the needed charm, and then some.

Was or was not Jenkins a slithering, duplicitous bastard? Student could answer that question right enough.

Having a wife who was Chairman of the Board of Regents — well, it didn't get more influential and establishment than that. Then, leading an on-campus life of protest and extreme left politics, screwing young women with long skirts and flowers in their hair. That face of him satiated, he would nightly motor across the Golden Gate Bridge to a world of privilege where money was the prayer rugs of wealthy and upscale manor houses sprawled.

And how did he do this? Jenkins' real skill was to cozen an old woman.

Student laughed and banged on top the steering wheel from the mirth this image conjured: Jenkins following some old crone, spinning fictions about how time had little or no effect on her holiness's external parts.

By Jove! Student took another —lustier hit — from the cognac, reminding himself to hold back some for later — going home. Anyway, this over-the-top New Year shindig offered nothing but cart loads of quality liquor. At these things, any soul with an iota of egalitarianism got shit faced to drive away the guilt of attending such a cauldron of privilege.

He knew these things.

Student reflected on his experience at banquets and dances at various officers clubs. Such a get-together as this one was going to be easy in comparison to military officers where rank was so almighty.

He felt especially prepped to promote both the play and the playhouse.

Student had numerous lines ready to impress, an easy thing surely. Most of these over-educated desk jockeys were ignorant as toads. They had no idea where a play like *The Lower Depths* fit regards the canon of twentieth century theater.

He put the Dart in gear, got onto the road and carried on.

The immediacy of tonight's social challenge activated an attack of memory, an intrusive disorder since it pertained to Debbie.

This was damned poor timing, but he could not stop it:

Student, though normally of a reserved nature, knew he was entertaining and witty in a social setting. Debbie was envious of this; hence, when he really got going, she would drag him away, perhaps realizing how slow-witted she was compared to Student.

In fact there had been such an incident at her father's country club ball. They argued about social drinking and a sense of decorum. She had insisted they go home early and that she drive. Student understood, for he was all for highway safety. They drove by boundless Iowa corn fields — probably her father's — then she unexpectedly turned into a small service road.

It was a sky-filling full moon on a hot summer evening, and Student thought she was in the mood for some passionate, sweaty necking. And perhaps even more.

She switched off the car and the headlights. Then got out.

They were inundated by a coursing illumination of moonlight and the extraordinary mass of lightning bugs swarming up, down and over the myriad of corn tassels.

She turned towards him — her dress was a gauzy blue but now seemed white in the lunar wash. She slipped from it then from her undergarments, reached down and took off her shoes and put everything neatly on the hood of the car.

Student was astounded — Debbie an indubitably modest, conservative young woman — laughed when she saw his mouth drop open. He needed no invitation; when he burst from the door, she ran off still laughing, disappearing in the cornrows — easily a dozen feet high.

He bolted after her but went sprawling, leapt up and was off à la Jesse Owens. This was the sort of foot race Student was bound to win! Her body — perfect in clothes — was flawless without. She sprinted ahead dodging and doubling back like an Olympian nymph, somehow always gaining yardage on the turns. Student realized his coordination was not up to snuff, even stumbling several times more.

Goddamn! Owens would be ashamed to know his autographed photo hung on the wall of such a fool.

The problem was, her experience in sweet-corn jungles exceeded his, and though he could hear her — she would laugh and call out — he would get off course. Eventually he ended up back at the car in time to see her slip back in her clothes.

He collapsed in exhaustion — the heat and humidity of the night overwhelmed. His clothes were soaked and covered with dirt. Hers, of course, remained spotless.

"There. Are we feeling a bit clearer headed now, Stu?"

He was just working up a reflective wave of loathing for such a dirty trick when he rounded a gentle bend and saw the veritable forest of Norfolk Pines lining each side of an extraordinary long driveway. The memory of his humiliation in the corn field was dashed away by the present.

There was an impressive iron gate, with an overhead arch and Mrs. Jenkins maiden name arrayed across in decorative iron letters.

Student had arrived! — at least at the gate.

He took a lung full of air, a last brace of cognac and closed the glove compartment with finality. *Now is the time, Student; now is the time.*

The driveway threaded through the pines, widened and described a large loop before a three-story mansion with outlandish Doric columns. "What was this place," laughed Student, "the set for *Giant?"* In the middle of the loop were scrupulously landscaped gardens, a tall fountain in the very middle. A great St. George's

Lion atop spewed water onto tiers — spotlights showed the water cavalcading down from one tier to the next, then into the main pool. Each spotlight had a revolving set of colored lens, adding that California touch.

Valets — wearing Chinese costumes — awaited, and he actually wasn't early at all, being third or fourth in line. His *Dart* stood out like a mud hen in a line of swans, but that didn't bother him in the least. With such a homely vehicle, as director of *The Lower Depths,* he was demonstrating a social ambiance reflecting his dedication to the project.

His valet — who not only wore Chinese costume, but was Chinese, or at the least oriental, went to get in his car on the left hand side, only to discover the Dart —whose former owner was a rural mailman — had a right hand drive.

The valet found himself staring at the dash on the passenger's side.

"A right hand drive?!"

The valet slid over, tight-lipped. After his Dart bounded off, Student found himself facing the fountain. Such a layout fascinated, and he walked into the garden area, and followed a path to the imposing fountain. There were dozens of goldfish in the final tier, a pond. They had veils of multi-colored fins waving about as they swam into the current: there were gold, white, black and mottled fish — not a one of them less than a foot. Small baskets of bread had been placed for guests to feed them. Like these fish feeling at home in water, Student felt fully braced for the social challenge facing him. He managed a clever grin — a private moment of confidence.

Time to get on with this mockery.

He walked towards the entrance, not breaking stride until faced with two men — again dressed as Chinese. They collected his invitation, and despite their eye makeup — these chaps were *not* Chinese — he noticed they took an extra moment's look at Student.

The double-doorway swallowed him and he bypassed two faux Chinese girls who were checking in coats and such. Student was initially greeted by a man bearing a tray of drinks.

"Is there an open bar?"

"Of course, Sir, actually three of them."

He would be damned if he'd slosh down this cheap stuff. He instead headed towards the closest open bar and ordered three-fingers of the Napoleon cognac, not even causing the barkeep to blink. Like Student, the man knew his French nectar.

Student took this as final confirmation that he was attending an exclusive gathering.

Musicians somewhere played Chinese music; Chinese animals of the Zodiac hung everywhere, and not likenesses you procured at a party or caterers wholesaler, but fine handmade figures.

All service people wore Chinese costumes. But the grandest nod of all to the theme of the occasion was a spacious cage elevated on a table in the middle of a central atrium: In it was a mammoth New Hampshire rooster — a breed his father and Student had raised years ago for the 4H competitions. He stood listening to someone explaining that the grand fowl was an ancient Chinese breed first described by Marco Polo in the gardens of the Great Kahn.

Student allowed a chuckle on that bit of garbage but he was not here for purposes agricultural; let the dummies think anything they like.

He needed to find the party's "nucleus." Every party had one. At this center the most important person or persons were surrounded by world-class lick-spittles. The ancient art of being the most slithering obsequious dupe in the room would be in Olympian mode.

Finding himself holding an empty glass, he diverted to yet another bar, got three fingers more of the same, and set out in search of this *nucleus*.

It didn't take Student long, for his instincts were on their highest setting. He walked into a spacious art-deco style room where all that could be seen were shoulders and backs — mostly male — and the pro-forma laughter of desperate people before the throne of power.

Within this circle, Student knew, was 'Caesar,' and he would find Jenkins and his wife holding court. He knew Jenkins would be fast on the uptake — to get Student's task out of the way and him gone.

He threaded his way in — meeting begrudging resistance from older, immaculately garbed place holders. They all held drinks filled with the fatuous bar do-dads such as swizzle sticks, olives or even bits of mint and cherries.

These ridiculous drinks were characteristic of gutless imbibers who couldn't tell a good cognac from a half-assed super-market imitation. And behind each drink was a shaven pan with a nose holding up a pair of spectacles. In short, Student was in the company of sycophants such as chancellors, vice chancellors, and chairmen of departments.

Emerging into the clearing he saw no Jenkins, but instead a woman sitting on a settee — by herself — her legs crossed, but wearing a short skirt that displayed an eye-filling set of legs; the rest of her was the same. Oh, what a great comedy this evening was becoming.

This woman, though no spring chicken, had been adept and monied enough to keep all her exterior parts very resistant to gravity. She had auburn hair, at least tonight, and eyes that at once looked up and caught sight of Student. Surely, he guessed rightly — his youth and obvious intelligence would stand out in this group of overdressed stiffs and weenie heads.

Though he never considered himself good looking or took part in such self-admiring delusions, compared to this pod of warthogs he was Adonis.

"And who is this, Richard Dear?"

Timed to the instant, Jenkins came through, gave her a drink — saw Student and introduced him. Then giving Student the old *"Do your best"* look, departed probably upon another wifely chore.

The totally, overwhelming irony of the evening — of the occasion, and perhaps even of the year — *this* woman was the elderly, old squint Jenkins had married, who everyone at school imagined used a walker or medical device to wobble into bed each night.

"Sit here, Mr. Patterson. Tell us, where did you get a name like Student."

He told the masses — the surrounding male Brahmin's collective hate and envy was enough to dissolve Student's innards, but they were screwed. Though a dozen smart remarks about his name bounced around inside diverse craniums, none risked being sarcastic. The miserable sots *had* to be polite.

She scooted a bit closer to Student, and at once he felt them drawn to each other — her sexuality emanated everywhere, and he sensed that if she had her way, she would disrobe, toss her legs around him and screw him right there if it weren't for the scandal of it all.

By God! There was a fine image.

There they would be: A daughter and great granddaughter of two former California Governors copulating on the settee with a chicken farmer's son before fifty or sixty guests.

One of the clueless academic trash heads yakked away

about his own drama program, but all topics of the theater vaporized for Student. He guided his hand beneath the derrière she so obviously presented. Her eyes looked at him with the knowing, intimate look of someone wanting more, and Student knew he soon would willingly provide.

He snaked his confident hand around the edge of her buttocks, slithered beneath the gossamer undergarment and then just gently, into the entrance of her golden fortress.

Goddamn, his system was dumping a male-driven flash flood of hormones into his blood stream, and Student's body vibrated — a supersonic jet breaking the sound barrier. Her voice in a somewhat raised but controlled voice asked,

"Young man, I would appreciate it if you removed your fingers from my vagina." Then she looked to the shocked onlookers and to several in particular, "Now show this little swine out of here."

Things can go wrong gradually or quickly, then there are disastrous events which proceed with the blinding speed and violence of a nuclear reaction: Student's ejection was of the last variety.

His brief transit to the entrance began as might a cat's carcass dragged along by a half-dozen bull terriers: He was yanked so hard upwards his coat was rent. While he was passed along, punches were driven down hard, and one outraged voice — its stentorian volume singular, *"By God, he violated Mrs. Jenkins, the drunken bastard."*

In angry disarray, the mob dropped him on the floor enabling them to kick — then yank him upwards again, tearing his coat completely off.

Student remained conscious — and in fact, his nervous system was so thoroughly anesthetized, he suffered the pummeling with surprising endurance. Then voices of authority made themselves known, and he saw different sorts of faces in the gaps between his attackers.

"Gentleman, we're security; this is our job," but the pause in the trouncing was momentary, and though carried in a direction of the front door, he still heard voices —their intent was continued deft frontier justice.

"Kill the miserable little swine!"

At that moment an amateur pugilist managed a roundhouse punch to his temple causing temporary blackness — a few stars — then images returned. And still the voices — those of authority — calling for calm.

"Just a little bit of excitement here folks — just a party crasher."

Student was hurled between the entry portals, rolled down the steps — then fielded rugby-style by at least three or four vengeful souls. By no means were they finished with him — these were the Righteous and would have his hide. He tried to fend off blows and kicks, but they rained down from all directions.

"This bastard sexually assaulted Mrs. Jenkins."

"Gentleman, this is our job, not for the guests."

Possession of his carcass was being fought over by professional security types and guests,

"To so outrage a woman we honor so! Here, eat this you little animal."

Another roundhouse glanced blessedly from his shoulder — then another on the top of his head.

"Oh, goddamn, I've dropped my glasses!"

"I think they're over here, Chancellor."

This sudden good fortune removed precise vision from Mrs. Jenkins' most pugilistic knight-errant, and the punches ceased.

"Gentlemen back off God damnit. We mean it! This is our job."

These voices were menacing — and at once only two individuals had him. His clothing continued to shed in handfuls as they pulled and yanked Student to his feet and gave him a punitive shake. There would only be a wad of rags to return to the rental agent.

Resistance was beaten out of him, and Student was resigned to whatever fate awaited. He was pushed — dragged when he fell — again yanked to his feet, then pushed through the garden to the fishpond,

"Here, motherfucker. Sober up."

He was tossed in with the goldfish. Student tried to sit and access air, but took in water, an unkindly hand pushed down again; again he struggled to the surface porpoise-style. He spewed fountain matter, coughing and retching. He was snagged and yanked from the water and left supine at its edge. A new voice entered stage right.

"What's the trouble here."

"He put his hand up the boss lady's pussy."

There was group laughter and some ungenerous humor at the expense of their employer.

"OK, finish the drunken bastard off and get him out of here."

Student was dragged to his feet, pushed — but along the way he vomited into the garden and pain was developing throughout his mauled body.

"OK, hotshot, they're bringing your car around. Then get in it, and get the fuck out of here."

He was pushed into the left-hand side of the Dart before they realized it was a right-hand drive.

"What in the fuck is this shit?"

He was then yanked out, half pushed, half dragged around and shoved behind the wheel.

Student struggled to see ahead, knowing that driving was going to take a semi-miraculous performance. The car door was slammed shut, and he fumbled, struggling to realize what he should do.

He looked out the window, one of the Oriental valets who grinned inward described a little circle above his head in mock-race official style.

When he realized he must punch the Dart into gear, he scraped pond weed from his hand for he had become a virtual swamp creature. When he did punch 'forward' the Dart clicked into gear, it set off more or less at .05 mph.

His body began to tremble from the trauma of the beating, plus his blood alcohol level was higher than a thermometer, regressing his motor skills twenty seven years.

He had become a three year old, learning to drive.

Student struggled to control the car from following its random-wandering/mode. He steered away seconds before the Dart rammed the fountain. He swerved onto the portion of the loop, but instead of going *away* he *went back* to the battleground. Driving into the war zone, he was greeted by the troop of australopithecines hired as valets. They took gleeful opportunity to pound on the top of his car, hoot primitive vocalizations and diverse invectives — even hurling gravel through the half open window of the passenger side.

"*Wrong way, you stupid bastard.*"

"*Somebody call the cops.*"

He took firmer grip on the wheel, steering around unclear figures. He abruptly recalled — it was night,

"*It is night, Student. You'll need lights to maneuver along the ¼ mile drive of trees.*"

His *Sober Voice* — always with him no matter how drunk he got — reminded him of the obvious. Yet the voice never helped in physical/neural functions to do practical things — like work the correct control.

But he tried.

The heater came on and as it had since purchase, commenced a grinding wheeze. On the second attempt, he pulled out the cigarette lighter — disgusted he tossed it out the window.

The third attempt did nothing at all. Ahead, vague outlines of oncoming objects loomed.

Abandoning the issue of lights he took the right turn he guessed avoided the solid objects — certainly Norfolk Pines — instead leading him between the column of trees towards the state highway.

A baffling problem ensued: Instead of two columns of pines there was only one, straight ahead, and he drove squarely into it, the first tree. Even at a crawl his head bounced off the steering wheel.

Beside him was a voice — or more logically — one person speaking, of all things, a good Samaritan.

"You've got to back up straight. Stop! Straighter yet."

The arcane push-button drive of the Dart became a sudden Godsend, for he could never work a handle or peddle.

He followed instructions; now there were two rows of trees. The helping voice had a less hostile tone; he felt a hand on his shoulder.

"Now, punch it and get the hell gone while there's time; they've called the cops."

The two rows of pines were a safety measure — had a farseeing designer intended them for soused drivers to navigate out to the state highway?

His central nervous system in team effort with his liver battled gamely to clear itself of the cognac. Student kept up forward momentum, yet saw that the pines were passing by with glacial speed. He gave it a bit more accelerator.

He was still not sure of the alignment, for he had not managed the lights.

Student wrestled the steering wheel, bringing one row of trees to the right hand and the other to the left. These trees were guideposts from the Gods!

Still, he must have lights. He tried again, and this time the wipers went on, and while groping for another control he noticed one of the rows going completely out of sight.

He steered — veered suddenly — and his head bounced off the roof of the Dart. The entire undercarriage emitted a violent metallic report, then a plain of grass and dirt spread before him. No trees!

What happened? What in the name of Jesus happened?

He took his foot off the accelerator, but the car did not stop — but eased on, a pilgrim of forward progress.

"Step on the brake, Student and punch it into neutral; you could be driving into the Pacific Ocean."

Student pounced on the brake sending his forehead forward into the wheel again. Perceptions whirled around like pigeons in a vortex while he fought to comprehend this outlandish situation. What hath God wrought?!

"Mr. Patterson. Get in. Get in."

His window was still open and out it he saw a Chinese woman looking at him, gesturing wildly. How could he know a Chinese woman? But, he was glad to see her.

"Hello, I'm in a bit of a fix."

"Mr. Patterson, the cops are coming. Now! Get out and get in here. We've got to get the hell out of here Now. Now! Do you understand me? They called the cops on you."

Cops! This night would end like it did with the disaster in downtown Saigon. He opened his door and fell out on his head.

"Oh, goddamn, you *are* fucked up."

He was helped to his feet, and trundled around with authority, stopping before a microscopically small door. He balked: Certainly he could never get in it. But he was not allowed to hesitate — instead his head was shoved down and ram-rodded into place, the door slamming behind him.

The Chinese woman hopped behind the driver's wheel and sped off, working madly at the gear shift and clutch. Student didn't think Chinese women were so strong.

"Jesus! Pray! I *can't* get stuck. You drove into a *pasture*. I don't know how you got over the ditch without using that little bridge. They called both the Sheriff and the California Highway Patrol. What in hell did you *do* back there, Mr. Patterson?"

She made the highway with a lurch, and stooped over the wheel hot-rodder style, bringing the tiny car to full speed. Driving with one hand, she removed costume makeup with the other and metamorphosed into an Occidental woman. When she looked over at him, he rubbed his eyes to clear things up, and sudden recognition slapped him in the face. It was Miss Exception herself, Jessica Bolton.

A thoroughly calamitous night.

"What did you do? Do you remember?"

"Miss Bolton, I believe?"

"Yes. And lucky for you. I recognized you in the middle of the troop of baboons who were beating the hell out of you."

"Yes. Lucky."

"The cops *are* coming, you know. Mrs. Jenkins had the head of security call both."

Even at this precarious moment, that seemed inordinately ironic, considering his driver. He chuckled lugubriously — the alcohol sloshed around a bit in his brain until he located the junction between sarcasm and snotty.

"You think you'll *know* any of them?"

"Not too shit-faced to be a wise ass, huh? Well, I'm doing *this* because I owe you for what that imbecile of a cop *did*. One more witticism Mr. Student Patterson and I'll push you out the door and leave you to your fate. I gave up an hour's wages to do this, plus we're not out of it yet."

There wasn't enough liquor in the entire country to camouflage female angst — she meant it,

"Oh God, here they come — the first of them."

Straining-booze impaired eyes and leaning forward, his head came to rest against the tiniest windshield in memory. Approaching were flashing red lights sweeping across field and hillside creating an uncanny stop/go panorama. Around the curve the patrol car loomed into view, and she pulled dutifully off the road when it smoked passed.

"OK. That's one. With Her Highness's influence, I wouldn't be surprised if dozens will come. What a bitch! I'll get off this road, and use the back way."

She slowed, down-shifted and the car — and it was a tiny car — labored up a considerable hill, Miss Bolton cursing under her breath for the stupidity of it all.

"What sort of a car is this. It is awfully tiny."

"To you, it is a magic carpet. You've pissed me off. So, just sit there." She looked at him and muttered something unintelligible, then, ". . . a guy screws around and that's that, a woman does so and the guy thinks he owns her, and then an arrogant creature like you *believes* him."

They were not getting along.

Student kept silent — resisting the nausea that now took over. He was beginning to realize the degree of despair which had catapulted him into the abyss of strong drink. He was washed up now.

Student didn't care — weeks ago he decided to leave that summer. To where? He did not know or care. What Student *did* care about was directing *The Lower Depths,* plus Milly suggested the BTWG might produce another before the end of May. Tonight he had let down all those who trusted him, and especially Milly who he respected above all others.

How could he tell her what happened? Student's brains — though still sputtering — began to function. Oh, what an absolute dumb shit he had been. He managed an anemic groan.

With the night ahead and the tiny car struggling uphill, the Gods belatedly took pity and extending a kind hand, touched his forehead. Student either passed out or nodded off. It didn't make any difference.

12.

Seers of Future Present

(Elder Men and Women, all wearing goat horns, hooves and wool-like robes.)

Oh, it is a sad time, Student. A fickle and heartless Aphrodite has hurled you into a landfill of fornicators and mind-numbing wankers. She will have her revenge for your shabby attitude towards womankind. You now have been thrust into such a fast lane, that we're afraid you'll copulate yourself into oblivion. Many souls have taken the big swan dive into the tar pits of Hades because of this daughter of ancient blood. But we have not given up! We struggle faithfully for you despite your dreadful propensity to screw yourself.

Student woke under covers. He looked up into the dark and felt he was in the grip of advanced hog cholera. He remembered Miss Bolton waking him just before crossing the Golden Gate Bridge, and determining that between them they had 85 cents for gas. There *was* no gas left in her Simca.

"Those goddamned valets tipped themselves", she snarled finding his wallet emptied and money gone.

Jesus, he thought . . . *a Simca. I didn't even know they were legal on highways.*

He kept quiet about her car. It was nip and much tuck reaching her home in San Francisco's Marina district and being shoved up the walk into her apartment.

He was beginning to sober having vomited a bit more at the service station. He wondered how much longer Miss Bolton's feelings of compassion might last.

Student slept for hours. He was laying on what felt like a couch under a blanket. He struggled with vertigo, but his digestive system by now was purged.

His memory began treating him to tiny snippets of the previous night's devastating moments, explaining the soreness and a bulge over his eye. In fact, the eye was nearly closed.

My God, those bastards were on me like hounds.

This Chinese New Year tumult was worse than his last time over the top: In Saigon his ten-day descent into dissipation ended when he had walked into a very posh European-style hotel naked. He was deftly nabbed at the front desk by a pair of Shore Patrolman.

Earlier that disastrous week he fell into Madam Lee's fishpond — actually, the canal — naked so his uniform was spared. Hence, after he drank and copulated himself out of funds Madam Lee kindly dumped him in a cab and the driver paid himself by stripping him of his clothes, all good military stuff. He then left him at the hotel.

At least the burly shore patrolman didn't beat the hell out of him. *"Lieutenant, you really made a week of it."* Perhaps they admired the courage it took to attain such abandon. Student proved, if it needed so, he still had the potential for social catastrophe.

Outside the blanket's blackness he heard snickering. A vast pain undulated over his body, forcing a groan of pathos. More snickering.

He eased the edge of the blanket up; sitting across from him sharing a breakfast tart were one or two of the most extraordinary little girls he had ever seen. They were dark complexioned, even in the half-light, appearing made from the finest porcelain — handmade exotic beauties.

Slowly, tortoise style, he poked his head from under the blanket.

This caused more snickering.

He blinked, trying to clear up this double vision, but it did not pass. He tried to talk, could not. Where in hell was he, Siam? Istanbul? They remained two — identical, then one tried to seize all the pop tart, and the other objected in a language he had never heard.

"*Share* the pop tart. It is the last one."

Miss Bolton's voice came from the right, then moved to front and center, looking first at him, then to the girls.

"These are my twin daughters, Lea and Bila. Don't look at them like they're freaks, Mr. Patterson. They're Ethiopian."

"Ethiopian."

They repeated this, happy with the word. Student struggled, resenting her presumption.

"I do *not* think them freaks, just extraordinary."

She pointed upstairs and rattled off instructions in the language — Student supposed Ethiopian, sending them off reluctantly; Student evidently made for intriguing spectator sport.

"They have school. It is Monday."

She took a keen look at him, and promising coffee went out of view — from the sounds of it, a kitchen. As if drawing a curtain on a closing act, he covered himself back up, but there was no hiding the previous night of social and professional travesty.

Under the blanket, his sins flapped about in the dark, bats looking for a deeper, darker chamber where they could hang it up for the night. But each chamber was filled with an outrage: Fishponds, righteous academics and security toughs, a hand reaching into a forbidden place, Simcas, police, gross intoxication, public humiliation. Then rescue by a cop-fornicator who evidently earlier in life practiced her sexual fancies with Ethiopians.

And with it, he had badly bruised the project at the BTWG and demolished his own reputation.

He groaned. There was a firm pat on his head from the outside,

"Open up, Mr. Patterson."

He found a mug of coffee placed carefully in his hand. He struggled to a sitting position. The twins appeared, dressed for school and were at once inspected by Miss Bolton, using the language of their native land. She switched to English and pointed to each,

"Now, from now on, until you get home and I tell you it is OK, only English, you understand?"

They nodded, but that was unacceptable, "No; say it in English."

"We understanded."

"No, We *understand*!"

There was a knock, and everyone went out of view momentarily, and after greetings and goodbyes, Miss Bolton returned, dragged a chair in front of him and sat Indian style on it sipping her coffee.

"OK. What in hell did you do? After saving you, I deserve the full story, if nothing more for entertainment."

"A political argument went very wrong. How long have you been back from Ethiopia, Miss Bolton?"

She did not allow him to dodge.

"Politics — baloney. They damned near killed you. You must be a tough nut. You know, you look halfway OK. By the beating you got, I thought there wouldn't be much left of you. Anyway, you're not going to tell me?"

"Vietnam. You might recall, is a topic that can easily get out of hand, especially if you support it."

"And you support it?"

"No. The others did."

"And you did not?"

"Correct. And I've served there, and shared my experiences. So it started."

She got out of the chair, reappeared, took up the same position; she ate — finishing off a pint container of yogurt causing instant stomach rebellion in Student.

After a spoon full, she shook her head.

"So, you're not going to tell me."

"I just *did*, Miss Bolton."

Sighing she hesitated, and reluctantly responded,

"We've been here just two years. Not quite. The girls turned six a week before we left. Their English is *really* coming along."

He sniffed the coffee — tested it, then sipped. She took each spoonful of the yogurt with a slip of her tongue, then drawing it in closed her eyes momentarily, paused, then another spoonful.

"I suppose you don't want anything to eat?"

"Oh, no thank you. I should go. I have to get my car back. I rather made a mess of things last night."

"By sticking your hand up Her Majesty's pussy?"

He looked at her; she didn't even glance up, but continued her yogurt.

"Then why did you ask me?"

"Just thought I'd see how you put it."

He took a braver sip of coffee and regretted almost everything he'd done during the previous 48 hours — which now put him in a terrible pickle. He didn't have car or money, and in fact, knowing the city like he did, wondered how to get back to his hotel.

She finished her yogurt, the tongue taking in the last of it — lapping a tad off the inside rim. It occurred to Student that under her robe there was nothing; it was made of thin material, and was tied loose at the waist with a blue sash. She was small, but very compact, and remembering her both in sloppy and fancy clothing, knew she was built — for power, as it were.

Yet her feet were tiny, and he was taking in her lower leg and the visible wedge of her upper thigh when he saw her peeking at him over the top of the yogurt container. She put the yogurt aside.

"You could be worse off, physically."

He sat up — yipped when it hurt.

"They had their way with me."

When she got up to take the empty container to the kitchen, her robe fell open more and Student kept his eyes right there. Returning she sat and looked steadily at him, as if appraising him for a fitting — or the oven.

"But despite that you still want me?"

He was angry and humiliated that she was right. He mustered the most available defense against this — this *hubris* of hers.

"A glance doesn't equal wanting, Miss Bolton."

"A glance?"

She smiled, reached over and drew back the blanket, took his coffee, set it aside and began to undress him, beginning with his trousers. She held her index finger up to her lips, and shushed him,

"Let me take the more active part — in view of the situation."

He watched, and his male animal yet possessed vitality within his semi-injured state. It was a wonder of natural history: millennia of primate evolution enabled the male to endure horrible combat yet have enough endurance to claim *Les femmes de combat* by immediately coupling with them under nearby bushes while emitting savage snorts and grunts.

She moved up and over *expertly*, and Student slid her robe down and off. Her eyes took him in — appraising each portion. And God help Student, but he marveled at her body and how effortlessly she commenced efforts, drawing him far in where he might never want out.

During the ensuing eight days Miss Bolton maintained her lead physically, but Student healed and was doing his best to catch up. The sex, done whenever their persons were proximate, was either spontaneous or planned but as close to constant as social niceties would allow. Their intensity matched a pair of ordinarily solitary Bengal Tigers busy making more giant kitties.

They, however, would not have thought it frenetic, despite there being very little talking but of the necessities. During this intermittent Saturnalia lives had to continue: For Student, rehearsals of *The Lower Depths* began, while Jessica maintained a busy evening schedule working for a high-end caterer serving very important people,

Student began to wear down in the later rounds: He was losing sleep, and despite increased food and liquid intake to fuel physical demands his weight loss was obvious.

"My goodness, Student; do you have the flu?"

Milly wondered after his health. She inquired only once

about the Chinese New Year party at Jenkins' then no more. Certainly she heard a hint of the sad facts, or worse — an entire exposition of events. But she politely desisted asking questions in view of his opaque response to her initial inquiry, *"Well Milly, there were hundreds of people there, and I was a bit overwhelmed by it all."*

He waited for the inevitable condemnation from Jenkins and the college — at the least in written form, but the sword of Damocles remained dangling over his head.

Meanwhile, the unquenchable couple pushed the throttle all the way open and kept at it. And never once were they caught *en flagrante* by (most importantly) the children or anyone else, in what was a world class achievement of discretionary screwing.

Close to two full weeks after the debacle it was time for his scheduled meeting with Jenkins, which included the progress of *The Lower Depths* at the Haywood Playhouse. He still had not heard a word from Jenkins but he had been busy.

Jenkins was arrested with Jane Fonda and other celebrity protesters before the Administration Building at Berkeley. The educator's presence during high-profile protests were prime activities. With the rich and famous present, he wouldn't get beaten into a heap by the cops who loathed the very mention of him.

But despite this schedule, when he showed up Jenkins had time to worry after Student's health.

"My God, Student, you look like hell. What do you have, mono or something?"

Student remained braced for just about any form of condemnation regards his outlandish — scurrilous behavior — with Mrs. Jenkins. He was ready to plead anything so he might continue directing *Depth.* This extraordinary experience stood out without question as the most discombobulating incident of his post-chicken farm life.

They began with his complete written report — both artistic and financial — it was a smooth professional review. Jenkins paged through while listening, betraying no emotions north or south. He asked a few cogent questions. Then he lost focus, and asked if Student had screwed Milly, raising the obvious question with Student that in the early planning stages of the grant, Jenkins had. Oddly, this bothered Student.

"Milly has become my best friend. Essentially she is my assistant, in addition to being the arts director, costume person and just about everything else. The project would be in hopeless shape without her."

Jenkins folded up his report, and looked slyly at Student. Rolling his office chair over to his door, he shut it, then looked coyly at Student.

"Now, tell me what the old girl *did* when you put your hand into her quim. What a *priceless* move. Oh, Student, I know you were drunk on your ass, but I'm proud of you. You know, half those slabs of humanity cozening her have been fucking her over the years, and not consecutively either. The old tart is damned good at keeping the one ignorant while she's screwing the other. So one imbecile thinks he's sitting in the catbird seat, and the other thinks the same! Oh what a cosmic fucking dance it all is."

Student had his apology readied — despite Jenkins' remarkable view of her activities, Student plowed ahead with rehearsed lines.

"Dr. Jenkins, I ask you for largesse — to forgive my behavior. Yes, I had too much to drink, and it overwhelmed. I hope you'll allow me to finish directing the play. I will of course resign my fellowship in June."

Jenkins raised both arms and waved a dismissive gesture.

"Don't be ridiculous, Student. I'm afraid those jealous

old fucks gave you quite a drubbing, didn't they? A mawkish competition between those decrepit walruses to see who might uphold her honor with the most vigor."

Student owned to their eagerness and almost allowed slip that the valets had robbed him. But he had slipped by this moment with stupendous good fortune so instead bade Jenkins farewell and got the devil out of there. In fact, he left Jenkins still chuckling over his wife's public violation.

He stopped for extra oxygen outside the building. Jesus Christ — life had become so awfully complicated for Student of late. Having this potential sword removed from over his head was a great balm.

Miss Bolton waited in the parking lot with the twins. He brought them to his favorite pizzeria. They sat in his usual booth. The twins intrigued him. For starters — he never saw anyone eat slices of pizza by holding the pointed end away from them — biting the base first.

And the two little beauties were a hit at the establishment. The owner called the young ladies over to the counter for a complimentary mint. This gave the mother time to ask a somewhat tardy question,

"You know, since we have been screwing in every nook and cranny larger than a telephone booth for two weeks plus a few days, couldn't we call each other by our first names? May I be so forward as to call you 'Student,' or do you have a shorter nickname? And Jessica is just fine for me."

So they continued the next afternoon in a different way. Instead of pawning the children off on their aunt and uncle who owned a limousine service, they continued to the beach. Though a cloudy, breezy day they parked off the highway and threaded their way between the dunes and found they had almost the entire place to themselves.

She and the children chased waves, and vice versa. Student pondered life's developments — for he was a long ways from the corn fields of Iowa, and surely the life view he learned there.

Now sex was a daily activity, in fact nearly focal. In contrast, certainly rural America — like rural Iowa — men drove about on tractors and much aware of sexual intercourse, yet spending most of their hours worrying about other matters.

Not Student. After receiving his letter-of-dismissal from Debbie — he at once became aware that his sexual background was so thinly sliced it probably rivaled that of Mother Theresa. Admission to a life of conjugal sex, he had accepted, was faithful adherence to propriety. All the abstinence Debbie had imposed upon him — and there had been a steady diet of that — turned to so much fool's gold via one letter. Debbie deftly ceased the brownie and cupcake stuff and had taken the big swan into intemperate screwing.

Now issues were very different.

"Do you think having sex five times a day is abnormal?"

Jessica looked startled when he'd asked this — as if he'd inquired if breathing, or food passing through one's intestines were normal.

"Only if you don't have the time and place, Student!"

And she enjoyed a wonderful laugh on his wide-eyed innocence.

He stepped willingly into all out whoopee. Though he too had tossed old ways aside, and moved towards the carnal in Saigon, he had suffered through the bad and now was staring a bunch of good right in the face. He earned it.

"Mr. Student. Explaining the ocean to us."

The twins free-fell into his musings — with an issue.

"Student, explain the ocean to us, *please.*"

Jessica corrected them — but both remained planted there,

evidently having some furious debate only properly addressed by a quick explanation of the planet's oceans.

Student drew a scholarly breath and began.

He summed it up with a review of the basics: The primary reason there was so much ocean and that all the oceans were indeed so deep and vast, was to give sufficient room for great whales to wander.

Student was pleased he fully explained things to their satisfaction — for the twins turned back, and resumed dragging a long piece of kelp parallel to the surf shouting directions to one another in Ethiopian.

"That was clever, Student."

He looked at her. Though wanting Jessica right here and now, he was beginning to see intelligent eyes and an alertness.

"You know Jessica, I should like to know who you are."

"I was thinking the same. You think stupendous sex and learning a bit about each other are mutually exclusive?"

"No."

Without a doubt there was a transition in progress.

She and the twins had an Easter dinner at San Francisco's only Ethiopian Christian Church, and though invited, he declined. He pried himself out of the Simca bade them farewell at the garage where he stored the Dart. He changed his mind about driving anywhere in the disgraced Dart, and instead walked back to his hotel.

He should have gone on a drive.

He was treated to unbridled bedlam at his hotel.

Mrs. Smith was finally sacked, and the Fong Brothers put their cousin Edwin Fong in her place as resident manager — clearly promoting the *A plus B Hotel's* priority in the world of

Fong. Edwin — mostly recently of Macao — began by posting a large, new sign in less-than-flawless English, none the less easily understood: He disallowed from the premises all liquor, tobacco, women, hot plates and anything hanging on a wall weighing more than eight ounces, and absolutely any pornographic literature and/or pictures.

He initiated a crash room inspection about a half hour prior to Student walking in. Outraged residents pursued a terrified Edwin back to the office where he was at once under siege. In fear of his life, he tried to shut the top part of the door, yet the besiegers held it open.

"No, not so fast. This isn't the county lockup, you slant-eyed little fuck."

"You don't Chinese gentleman call slant eyed, you som'bitch," then he erupted into Cantonese with Portuguese sandwiched in, and got down into serious international name calling.

An elderly man — the *A plus B Hotel* sage, a man — once a 'heavy hitter' in major real estate deals until a divorce and strong drink brought him low — was on the pay phone letting the Fong Brothers know of this mayhem.

Student diverted, scooped up his mail from its slot, ascending to the 3rd floor. He was now a veteran at shutting out the ambient noises in the hotel. Behind the door of his room there was an afternoon interlude when the mail allowed him a brief visit to the conventional world of family cheer and fresh air.

Anyway, *Depths* rehearsals loomed in less than an hour and a half and he had no patience with the insurrection in the hotel.

He was facing dicey situations in the rehearsals: Freddy O'Malley was a bully with the younger, less experienced Thespians, especially in a play he had been in several times.

Unfortunately for Student, O'Malley lacked the talent of some of the younger actors but that didn't bother him at all.

Clashes ensued. Milly tried her best to intercede, but O'Malley overpowered her too, and plowed on, usually causing Student to recede into his Navy Officer/Director mode of being authoritative, not his style at all. And in the middle of all this, Milly broke her arm on her apartment house steps.

"I'm going to definitely complain about the stairs, Student — no lights at all."

Student assumed she lived with O'Malley, or vice versa, and O'Malley evidently would have preferred that. He had growled,

"My place is lit like a fat cat's luxury suite compared to that dive of yours Milly."

She demurred and shuffled some scripts around one-armed style. Student tried to cheer her up by saying something stupid about her breaking an arm instead of a leg, and it fell flat.

Well, he tried. Now he had the mail to enjoy — and he withdrew from the world of hotel insurrections and worries about bullies and such.

Removing a fresh, mailed copy of *The Weekly Worker* he wondered who at the BTWG was so considerate to provide him with a subscription, now putting him on all FBI watchdog lists. This copy hid letters, stuck in the middle of the fold. One was from his father and another with a handwritten address — the writing he knew at once. It was from Debbie.

Student sat upright; the uproar became audible again — including resident invectives raining on Edwin Fong.

He braced himself for ugliness, opened her letter, gave it a snap to unfold the page, and read:

Stu:

I want to tell you that it was not my intention to inveigle myself into your family especially in view of

our parting-of-ways. But circumstances which you know came to pass just caused it to happen, most of them being on the account of my father's attitudes. And, of course, mother will always follow suit, agree or not, for she considers that "her job." This ordeal caused her agony, and for that I cannot forgive myself.

But my point here, is to inform you that I was very up front with your Aunt Lila and your parents about precisely what I said to you in my last letter, that is I accused you of very stupid things that I now regret. So, my purpose here is to apologize for that — and to say how wrong I was. You are a good human being and would not harm anyone.

Stu, I know you, and want to assure you I don't need rescuing. I am not a fair maiden locked in a golden tower, but an ordinary 28 year old woman who went to a week-long rock concert without her prescriptions. I do have my teacher's certificate, and when things settle here, I will go to an area and start over, hopefully teaching. It appears now my Aunt Lulu in Maine will give us temporary housing.

Wherever I go, I will take my beautiful daughter Juanita Beverly with me. She is now three weeks of age, and I will love and be proud of her forever, and I don't care what the world says. Though, God forgive me, I am not without hard feelings I will grow out of it.

I am very glad to hear of your new love-in-life, the theatre, though it certainly figures. Be well, Stu.

Regards, Debbie

Student put the letter aside, and endured another ground loop in his global orientation, plus felt a genuine swine for thinking Debbie would never tell his parents and Aunt Lila about her accusation of murder.

Juanita Beverly: He had visions of an infant in a bassinet with ribbons and castanets, ready for the Flamenco circuit. This vision was quickly followed by Debbie nine months and three weeks ago doing rounds with an electric mariachi band under the bleachers.

And just what this add-on about hard feelings? Someone in the mariachi band, a faux love god with a necklace of Egyptian who-haws, or *him* — Student.

Well it had damned well not be the latter.

He became angry, guilty, caring and overall soft around the gills and conscience.

Student looked at his copy of the *Weekly Worker;* on page one was a photo of a man shaking his fist angrily at police and strike breakers. Student had equal right to shake his fist at many injustices. If he did so, he would get a sore arm, possibly risk it even falling off at the elbow.

He felt the nearly irresistible urge to scream something — anything — when there was a knock at the door.

'*Jesus Christ!*'

He did not want, now or ever, part in hotel politics. He sprang with a bit of excess to order them away, opened it and found himself staring at Davy Boy who had embarked on a semi-drinking spree. Though not at his screaming-at-the-moon stage he was unsteady. He read dutifully from a message slip,

"*Student: I must stay in my apartment for 48 hours for the arm to begin mending properly. I have three completed costumes and a half dozen hand-modified scripts. You may pick them up however late you like, or early. (Milly).*"

Davy Boy took out a bottle of vodka politely offering him a hit. Student declined with equal civility. He took his visitor by the shoulder and guided him to a chair and sat him down.

"Did she screw the arm up again?"

"No. I, in point of fact, field set it initially. But she didn't go to the ER, the dummy."

"*You* set it?!"

"I was a medic in Korea. But by the time her arm started throbbing, it was late, you know."

As drunk as he was, Davy Boy spotted the fresh copy of the *Worker* at once; he gestured towards it and Student motioned that he was welcome to it.

While picking it up, he offered,

"You know Student, I'd watch Freddy O'Malley."

"I watch him too much already — like during rehearsals."

"He thinks you want to hump Milly. Can't imagine that — homely as she is, poor woman. That's why he can treat her like shit, you know. "

He stuffed the paper in his back pocket, struggled up and turning 180 degrees with wooden-like precision, raised a hand in farewell,

"OK, nice chatting with you Student. Helluva guy, you are. A real intellect", then completed his dignified exit.

Student looked at Milly's note and reassured himself Milly would never tell O'Malley or anyone of the week they swept aside petty bourgeois barriers.

But the Feds knew of it, the Stalinist bastards.

Student experienced a grinding in his intestines imagining O'Malley's ham-sized hands around his throat.

What ever happened to Student's long-ago desire for normalcy? He had expected mellowing years of peaceful, quiet accommodation with only minor pitfalls such as dentist bills and mortgage payments for an extraordinarily ordinary home.

Someone had stolen Student's yellow brick road.

The next morning he took the trolley to Jessica's with a halfway stop at Milly's to pick up the material for the play. He refrained from taking the Dart if he were to remain in the city. After all, at Jessica's they would be staying indoors.

While watching the rain spattering against the trolley's windows, Student replayed the rehearsal the night before: He was relieved when O'Malley didn't show — his first absence — and his readings were taken up by his understudy, a strapping twenty-year old named of Sterling. Student was not as confident with Milly absent. Likewise, the cast missed her, asking about her injury which he could not answer fully.

One fact was clear: The Guild's Sergeant At Arms seemed a poor choice for medical treatment. Why had Davy Boy — of all people — set her arm in the first place?

Student found Milly's apartment via the map on the back of her note. It was fifty paces from the bus stop. He confronted the address somberly while holding his umbrella point to ground. He checked it twice against the note: *150 ½ Marston.*

Her residence had distinctive qualities: It was entirely contained at street level beneath a massive set of stairs — an ascending entrance to what decades before was a great post-fire Victorian mansion, now converted into a warren of suites occupied by wannabe social climbers. No flower children here.

Her half-digit number was embossed above her door, a shorter-than-normal portal. It was made of iron, and only creatures like minotaurs or gorillas could gain entrance without a key or welding torch. When he knocked Milly opened it at once, welcoming him with a hopeful series of apologies for poor housekeeping.

It was actually, she explained, a storage space converted years before into a studio apartment: The single room began at the highest point of the overhead staircase at a paneled wall, then squeezed down foot by foot to where the stairs met the sidewalk. In short, it was shaped like a giant wedge of cheese, save there was a small bathroom burrowed into the far side. It was triangular living at its finest.

Student was unable to hold his peace.

"Milly, these are the most extraordinary quarters I've ever seen, including those on board ship."

"Oh, but it is only 45 dollars a month, Student. Sit! It can accommodate anyone regardless of their height: From just several feet, up to nine. Just think of its versatility."

This was a rare entry to humor.

"But there aren't any windows, Milly."

She knelt on the floor and holding out her arm with the cast, then putting the tunics and scripts into a waterproof bag — one armed style.

"Why did Davy Boy have to set your arm?"

She straightened, and paused before tying up the bundle. She looked over the top of her glasses at Student — librarian style.

"Student, you aren't in the process of feeling sorry for me, are you? Feeling sorry for people is wasteful; the *struggle* against economic oppression is the key. You see, there is a *mammoth* ideological distance between feeling sorry for a situation and struggling to change it," she looked upward briefly, perhaps recalling recent contemplations, ". . . I just think this concept is far easier for women to comprehend than men since it deals with generational oppression."

Student mentally backed away from these issues like he would a basket of cobras. He still gazed at this singular living space: One wall was entirely of books; in front of it a reading light was on beside a Paleozoic-vintage easy chair. A massive book lay open upon it. Against the other wall was a sewing machine and drawing board. The bed was scrunched into the area where the stairs met the floor. One couldn't have screwed in that bed unless they were giant flatworms or possibly emaciated midgets.

Overhead, apartment residence scurried down the stairs off to work — the sharp 'tap, tap' of high heels, and the 'thump, thump' of flat-sole shoes.

She had not answered his question about her choice of medical treatment. Milly offered tea. Student knew Jessica had sent the girls off to school about 30 minutes ago and tea paled compared to getting there. Still, diplomacy and fellowship, if not taking precedence over heart stopping sexual gymnastics, at least begged some respect, even if only a few minutes.

So, Student had tea, but alerted her of his impending appointment.

She talked while it steeped.

"This is why Ruth cannot visit me, or why her father limits it. You know, don't you, that I cannot leave the United States — no passport. It was taken away. It has made being a mother very hard."

It was a case of the father's sins visited on the offspring — in this case Bomber Rothstein's notoriety and grand masterly skills in the field of explosives. The Feds had brought pressure down on Milly's older sister, herself, and daughter.

"If it weren't for Ruth's father's ministerial position in Israel, Ruth would be completely unable to visit," she handed over the tea and said, "I know you stand well with your government, you being a military officer and all, but I must tell you Student: My experience has shown how unfair your government can be — very unfair."

Student wanted to pursue matters, especially her notorious

father and perhaps how she had encountered motherhood by an Israeli politician. However, Student knew the topic of her father caused Milly to adamantly defend him — to remind that stories about him were folklore.

"*Daddy never harmed a person in his life. He is a master of his craft and a wonderful teacher*", Milly told one of the players who read of her famous family connection.

After tea — with her kind instructions on correct bus connections to the Marina — Student rode along on a decrepit, diesel-belching bus holding the parcel in his lap.

Student's musings fell upon the unique layout of Milly's abode. His memory brought back Milly's first explanation for her fall — "poor lighting" on her apartment's stairs. It occurred to Student there were no steps entering or exiting Millicent Rothstein's apartment. It was at street level.

Dark matters crept over him.

He had a mutiny on his hands. Student strode the quarterdeck like Ahab, contemplating *The Lower Depths* cast, minus Freddy O'Malley and Milly. It was in fact, Milly who engineered the gathering agreeing to decoy O'Malley away, and be absent herself.

Like a good First Officer on a navy ship, Milly stood between the cast and the captain/director, handling complaints as they arose. But, it went too far, and involved mostly O'Malley, who the cast assumed was Milly's main squeeze.

The cast began their complaints with the usual fears: *The Lower Depths* was as audience worthy as watching cement dry; also, it took about as long. Certainly any audience not actually glued to their seats — or paid to sit there — would flee sometime in act one or two cursing the entire cast.

They, however, liked and respected him, and in fact several of the younger cast members had asked him to have sex during lulls in rehearsals. This Student understood as a good sign of amiability.

He did his best — mutinies in any form were deadly business. He began as any scholar might. Student was in his element.

"Now Milly has explained; *I* have explained, the time and setting of the play and its social significance, and why an organization like the Butchertown Writer's Guild would debut such a play in their new playhouse. We all must learn that as theatricals we cannot always participate in dramas we find enjoyable or we ourselves would see. However as a professional, it is my responsibility to direct a play doing my best. As actors, it is the same. The show is the thing, always."

This was the timeless contact of all in the theater, and he had settled that rather well — he had to admit. But the real complaint wasn't aired yet.

There were eleven cast members around 21-25 years of age, and three old timers form the Guild, including O'Malley. It was an old timer who spoke up — a shabby, politically wise silk screen artist named Eddy. He rolled his smokes with one hand and had the strange habit of using his cupped hand as an ashtray.

"Fact is Student, Freddy carries on like an asshole."

A quickly stifled cheer; then nods and mumbling.

Sterling, O'Malley's understudy and who proved to be an unusually talented actor added,

"He never seems to be happy — you know. We should be happy."

And this gave Student his exit line: Student thanked the cast, gave them a zestful talk, and vowed to talk with O'Malley.

"We must have good fellowship on set. We open in a little

more than three weeks."

After the rehearsal, he noticed Simon Conners in the office. Knowing the old man overheard the meeting Student looked in. Next to Milly, he admired Simon the most. He was loading his pipe and just topped off a pot of tea with an ancient blue-enameled saucepan that lived full time on his hot plate.

"Careful with Freddy. Since jail, he's gotten more combative."

"I can see that."

"He was different back when he was Bomber Rothstein's apprentice — with the old Labor Socialist party back around the start of WW II." He poked the tea pot, slid a cup across the table to Student. "As a kid Milly got a crush on him— but he's different now. She's different now. Hell, we're all different now and it is not a good difference. The Nixons, Dies, McCarthys — those of us they didn't put in prison or chased out of the country, they made nervous messes."

Simon puffed on his pipe contemplating what Student knew was a hard political past.

They were alike, however, in having detailed discussions with a minimum of talk; hence, Student learned things in a most concise way with no malarkey included.

"So Student, what about this theater stuff? It is new in your life, right? I thought you were going to be a professor. Teach Shakespeare."

Student contemplated two cubes of sugar sink into the tea and dissolve, rather a symbol of his Ph.D. plans.

"I'm absolutely taken with theater, and plan to pursue it. I discovered something: At school there are fliers advertising for assistant theater directors here and there around the country. I'll apply. I am applying. No more professor stuff; I really ran off the academic track at that New Year's party."

"Jenkins told us. He thought it was funny — but it shocked hell out of Milly."

The cycle was complete. The person he respected most learned that somewhere inside he limped along with an ugly flaw. Student's behavioral acrobatics while in his cups were getting incrementally wilder — even unlawful.

Most who did such deeds under-the-influence usually begged off by claiming a well-timed black out. But Student could not — he remembered it all.

He thought Saigon was his nadir; it was not. Events celebrating the Year of the Rooster accomplished that.

"Fact is, Simon, I shouldn't drink to excess. I tend to wildness."

Simon took his pipe out, eyes widened,

"*Tend?*"

"Well, do. *Do* get wild."

Trudging back to the hotel it occurred to Student he had unexpectedly aired a plan for the immediate and near-immediate future. He had no doubt about the theater. Secondly, he finally claimed ownership of his alcohol induced wing dings which seemed to be occurring biennially since high school.

"Stu, I wish you would never allow yourself alcoholic beverages to excess."

Debbie had voiced this years back, but he never saw the need of life-long vows in view of the intermittency of the missteps.

"Nobody is perfect, Debbie," was his defense, but one day she confronted.

They were lazing about their favorite haunt along Thrush Creek and she countered with, *"It is not a matter of perfection."*

And back then the topic politely went away with an intolerably hot Iowa summer night, perhaps gobbled up by one of the giant catfish in the creek.

At the *A plus B Hotel* he had three letters: One each from his parents, and this time — one from Aunt Lila. News from home.

Why did life proceed with such irritating speed; could there not be a 'time out' while Student got this beans and weenies in a row, drama-wise?

For starters, he had to craft a return letter to Debbie, and it had already been a month, which might explain the letter from Lila. Was he being rude and/or righteous and/or unforgiving?

Stretching out on the bed, he moaned aloud, *"And just who in hell side is Aunt Lila on, for God's sakes?"* He kicked his shoes off, hoped they crushed a roach or three when they hit the floor and fell asleep almost at once. Slipping away, he allowed that mail could wait. It could really wait.

13.

Seers of Future Present

(Dressed in Russian peasant garb)

Student, just by making a few good decisions at this stage, don't think you're going to weasel out of this mess. For starters, it has been decreed by the Ancients that you are to blame for everything that has happened to Debbie. You misled her — even lied, and have lied to yourself about it.

If you completed your Navy time on land as you said you would, you and she would have not been separated. So, when you opted to play Popeye the Sailor Man and have fun, she went to Wisconsin. There she fell under the influence of a big hippie by the name of Issac Waldstein from upstate New York, son of Herbert Waldstein, the Donut King.

Then, after that randy, fork-tongued devil took his pleasure with her, the hopelessly naive Debbie was cast out upon a stormy sea of popular culture gone bonkers on every mind-altering substance known to man and woman. Before she wised up, the great but fickle Aphrodite took her amusement.

You have the relentless Furies on your trail, and those female immortals never let

**a lying, double-dealing male off the hook.
Student you must realize — see — your
clear path. If not the consequences will be an
unspeakable mess.**

Jessica Bolton knew that at the most, in five years she would be a successful novelist. She just sold two short stories to big-name magazines and had a literary agent in New York. She planned to move back to New York City; after all she was born there.

Now she was angry, for her plans were akimbo. Student arrived a few minutes before the twins went to school. Jessica dispensed not a 'hello' or even a smile.

After the children were off Jessica closed the door brushed past him, her face a scowl. In the kitchen she tossed a few breakfast utensils into the sink.

"Well, chances are better than even I'm pregnant, Mr. Student."

Student eased himself down at the table and thought frantically about what he should **not** say, **not** do and how **not** to look.

Unfortunately, this did not tell him a damned thing about the positive: What he should say, do and what non-judgmental countenance to assume. Jessica was a fireball of the first water. She moved out of the kitchen like a bantam-weight in the opening round, standing over him, arms crossed.

"Oh, this is going to really impress my in-laws when their widowed sister-in-law starts popping out illegitimate children. Coptic Christians are really super conservative." She spun on her heels and lamented, "Oh, Jesus Christ I had been so ***goddamned*** careful."

Student's mental rolodex spun like a dervish, but could not

find a fitting place to stop. But — he *had* to say something.

"If the chances are better than even, then there are chances you are not, right?"

She muttered something he couldn't catch.

"How did your husband die?"

"What in hell difference does that make? Christ almighty!"

She pushed the toaster oven even with the wall, shrugging,

"Anyway, he didn't die; he was executed-murdered- by the FRD, but that is history. This is now."

She began to pace, stopping to look down at him, nodding as if dictating an indictment against the heavens.

"My father was Ambassador to Ethiopia and I ran away with a military attaché. My racist father made things very hot for my husband by claiming through formal channels that he abducted me. What a mess."

Finally, Student thought of a good true thing to say — both in timing and fact.

"I will stick by you no matter what, Jessica."

She stopped, swiveled and stared—a thoroughly disagreeable stare,

"I don't want *No Matter Whats*! Fuck your No Matter Whats."

She dashed upstairs and didn't speak to him for three hours. He knocked at her door, and she said to leave her alone — not to get out, but to leave her alone.

Actually, by eleven a.m. or so, he put all his work and such back in a case he kept there. He could get angry too, and had. Going to the foot of the stairs, he announced his departure, turned his back on silence, and left.

What was this madness? Had the whole world gone gunnysack during the same week? He wandered down to the pier and sat, glaring out at Alcatraz, a superb metaphor at the moment.

Just what sort of metaphor, he didn't know, but it would become clear, the dark ones always did.

With the available time, he set about crafting his response to Debbie next morning. But first he reviewed his last dispatch of letters from the Iowa war zone. His Aunt Lila's quasi-admonishment was fresh in his mind.

". . . she labored over her letter to you a long time, and consulted no one prior to mailing it, though I knew what she was doing for she had to get your address from me."

Lila went on, explaining how Debbie's family's dissension was expanding: Debbie's mother was now sneaking over to see her grandchild, and when the father found out he forbade it, and the mother continued anyway — the first rebellious act of their marriage. The father declared a "legal separation" and moved his wife of 37 years into his former farm superintendent's house.

Family warfare was ugly and gaining steam each day. Lawyers lurked. Relatives buzzed, even a minister or two came sniffing around. *"In all, it has been a challenging spring,"* Lila concluded.

In noted contrast, his family was declaring a ticker-tape parade, at least spiritually.

In the middle of all the spring confusion, Student's father proclaimed total victory in his quest for the self-sustaining chicken farm. He decided to sell the farm and move not to Florida, but to St. Nevis and Kitts, which he read about in *Poultry Today*. There he would turn out his textbook on chickens, and put the entire industry on its ear when the poultry world got a scholarly load of what he'd done.

His mother had told Student in *her* letter, that it would be wonderful to finally get out of the hard, cold farm winters;

however, she did not care what they said in *Poultry Today*. She was not moving to a foreign country because she feared another war in view of the present international situation.

She and his father were in current negotiations, which were — like all their disagreements — ardent, making for lively evening debates with two worn sets of encyclopedias as referees.

Student decided upon specific 'no declare' items in his response to Debbie: That he was involved with another woman. To suggest, infer or hint (not a damned syllable) that he perhaps wanted to see if they could resume. Also *when*, or even *if* he was going to visit Iowa in the foreseeable future. And lastly, equal to a lunatic suggestion for reconciliation, would be Student taking any responsibility for her disastrous decisions and their aftermath.

Why should he validate her immaturity with any measure of gallantry?

He carefully wove an avuncular, even brotherly tone. He complimented her for telling his parents and Aunt Lila the truth about both what she wrote, and how she was sorry for that.

He mentioned his newfound love of the theatre, and that it was going well, which for the most part it was. Student knew his future would contain more theater. He signed off with a concluding salutation of good, but respectful fellowship.

It was a masterpiece of temperate prose. So, enough of Debbie.

Now he was confronted with Jessica's super-heated bolt from the blue.

Student braced himself and took an assessment and update of his situation: His cast held a near-mutiny; he had a "talk" coming up with a former Federal prisoner who was a violent man twice his size. Additionally, this same person might have broken his friend's arm, who was also his closest and intimate advisor. Furthermore, his future as a scholar was over, and that of a fledgling director was unsure. And at the moment, his current girlfriend thought she was pregnant by Student and wouldn't talk to him.

Jessica's news didn't astound, or in fact shock him:

Student had wondered — if for only a few stray seconds — that any contraceptive method could successfully offer its user safely after a hundred-plus sexual acts within 90 days. It was like expecting to repair an eighteen wheeler's tire with *Elmer*'s glue.

No, he would definitely not say that — the part about the glue.

If he was going to get the stuffing beat out of him, that would be first issue, possible fatherhood second. Indeed, the first outcome might cause Student to reappraise the second by medical necessity.

He called O'Malley and arranged to meet him alone at Big Lena's All Star Café, perhaps impeding him from committing mayhem before witnesses. Student specifically asked him to come without Milly.

Actually it proceeded well: Freddy O'Malley dipped a donut into his coffee and listened rather patiently, asking if Milly was either behind this, or a part of the group complaint.

"No. Of course not, Freddy. I'm the director."

"You are. You are."

They talked away at the edges of a few scenes, and suddenly Freddy asked,

"How old are you, Student?"

"30."

"I'm 54. I grew up in the Depression. I grew up in the

lower depths, even Milly was just a little girl then." Abruptly the furnace door fell open. O'Malley leaned over; human eyes shouldn't show red, but O'Malley didn't know that. ". . . So this bunch of kids are *play-fucking-acting* being on their ass, I'm re-creating it. See?!"

And he got up and walked out, waving something of a farewell to Big Lena, who looked on wearing a worrisome grimace.

Student was left with his coffee and pie, but supposed it might have been much worse. But, what the hell? He resumed eating the pie. Lena relaxed, bringing her tiny hand across her brow.

"Where's Milly? Her boy has blood in his eyes. What you tell him?"

"Oh, something to do with his part. You know."

"Give me a heads up next time you got bad news for O'Malley. I would serve your pie on a paper plate. Goes down the gullet easier in the event our boy goes postal."

She remained serious for a few second, then engineered a smile.

The pie stuck in his gullet while he slouched back to the Haywood Playhouse. There he found Davy Boy playing cards with Simon. Seeing a light under the curtain, he went back and found Milly working away at piece of scenery.

He told her about his meeting with O'Malley. And O'Malley's anger.

She wore a Whistler's Mother smock when working, and in duller light, would have been a look-alike though she lacked a white bonnet. She put aside a small saw and looked him over — a worried assessment.

"He is very into the socialist movement, meaning from a standpoint of activism. Aggressive activism. "

"Does he get —" Student fished around for a term to couch the harshness of his question, but nothing new came to him — "aggressive with you?"

Eyes narrowed at once; he had gone too far. Milly didn't look anything like Whistler's Mother now.

"You mean, as hitting me?"

"I mean as in breaking your arm."

"I broke my arm falling down the stairs."

"You don't have stairs."

She straightened and secured a solid eye-lock on him, remembering too late her fabrication. Yet Milly was not slow witted, "I lied because it was his stairs; ladies do that to keep their —" she paused and lowered her voice — "intimate lives to themselves."

"Why then, did O'Malley say at the same moment his place had stairs that were 'really well lit' — you know, to back up your story, he screwed up the story you're using now."

Milly stood, tossed the screwdriver down and for the first time since he knew her, fumed. He braced, backing down a pace. Student feared her more than O'Malley. She became imposing.

"Student! This is none of your concern, and you *don't* cross examine friends."

She shrugged off the smock and tossed on her street coat.

"*None whatsoever.* A socialist woman is first, last and always self-sufficient, and doesn't require men folk to be chivalrous — or anything bourgeois like that. Bourgeois being the operative word."

And pushed the curtain aside and huffed off.

Student surrendered to what was a thoroughly nasty day. He took the stage door out, passing a bit distant from the card players; however Simon raised his head and pausing before slapping down a card assured.

"Next day gotta be better, Student."

Davy Boy was always agreeable when it came to Simon.

"Fuckin' A."

Student navigated the streets of butcher town with the neighborhood theme walk — downcast. Did this mean he was being drawn permanently under the pall? He turned into the alley, a short cut to the hotel entryway.

Student reminded himself he experienced a most withering day, and should not allow it long term residence. He caught fresh resolve, and took the stairs two-at-a-time, wrapped around the turn on the way from the second to the third, but saw the note in his mailbox. He took it, and in his room turned on the light and read. He wasn't surprised.

"Student: Please trust me and stay out of it. I'll be OK. The play opens in less than three weeks now. I'm sorry. (Milly)

He put it aside, and climbing between the sheets felt lonely. And it was on overall feeling, for he moved along his present life with an illusory ambiance. Little he did was anything he had planned, not even close. Was it not proper to plan things before doing them?

A warm breeze reassured, spinning a most welcome sleep around him. And a dream came upon him of his father, the visiting balm regards the person he missed the most.

His father was happy, as he usually was. Student and he were each walking a chicken on a leash along a pristine St. Kitts shore. His father convinced his mother to retire there. It was the custom in the tiny island nation to take chickens on walks, as they did in Iowa. This was the selling point for his mother.

Student could not remember them taking chickens for walks. His father gently corrected, *"Oh Student, we did it all the time. Don't you remember?"*

During their constitutional Student and his father greeted

other evening promenaders who were also walking their chickens.

"Upon St. Kitts and Nevis," his father pointed out, "walking one's chickens is a powerful contributor to peace of mind."

Student was informed by Jessica they had saved at least 400 dollars and possibly more.

"A safe abortion in San Francisco is a lot, but in Mexico it is only 250 dollars, but you've got to get there and back, and all that."

Jessica was not pregnant after all but was tardy enough to prompt a plan B. This plan made him aware, or at least recognize, that he had begun fantasizing about Jessica and the twins.

Her plan B knocked his fantasy life akimbo. Visions of apple pie and parenthood were a definite residue of much earlier contemplations, a misty residue of fluffy pie crust rolled from harvest picnics and corn husking.

Jessica's plan communicated abundantly that the Ethiopian father of the twins given time and place somehow qualified for fatherhood; Student, thank you, did not. His function now centered on being a knowledgeable, considerate male body appropriately equipped and operational. Sort of a "pump up and hump" device a busy woman might buy.

Goddamn! Without warning his ears went back and he experienced pangs of nastiness. Student held on tight, keeping these cynical musings locked inside. Jessica eyed him — trying to catch the thoughts behind his gaze. There were suspicions.

"Student, you didn't want to be a father, did you?"

"Hadn't thought about it, actually."

This was reliable slither-speak. Why should Jessica believe that Student would want children? What in hell did she know about him? She knew a man who directed social dinosaurs in an overwhelmingly bleak play. Who provided evidence of public incompetence by getting sloppy drunk and being tossed into a fish-pond. And in the process getting so badly pummeled it required Jessica to effect a risky but effective rescue.

No! For a creature like Student to procreate would be a violation of even the most slapdash eugenics. What might happen if he passed along genetic material tangled with strands of misanthropy?

After picking the twins up, they went on promenade down the Embarcadero. Student told them stories about ships while they tried to convince him to become an Ethiopian.

"For we say Mr. Student, we are princesses and someday will return to our kingdom and make you a movie star."

Indeed, he assured them they were princesses, but he thought becoming an Ethiopian movie star might be beyond him.

So, the fantasia that Student could help rear such an intriguing brace of children was a mental dalliance of the first water. Perhaps Student's personal phantasmagoria was an emotional attempt to escape the ambiance resulting from directing *the* landmark 20th century play of social reality. After all, Maxim Gorky hadn't been trying to cheer people up.

This faux family promenade described a loop back to her car, and once again Student invited her to tonight's rehearsal, assuring her they were getting better each night.

"No, I think I'll wait until opening night, and get depressed all in one sitting."

Each Ethiopian princess gave him a hug and Student wished he were going with them.

He experienced a need to brace himself for tonight's

rehearsal. Why? Student lapsed into thinking fondly of his time at sea — the wonderful boredom and predictability. There were clear duties, watches to mind then a retreat to your bunk to immerse into the most amniotic of sleeps.

His last transit of the Pacific after his shameful wing-ding in Saigon proved the palliative nature of the sea: Even polluted with diverse drugs and ointments to cure his collection of whore-house diseases his slumber was total. All the ugliness heaped upon him by Fates were ameliorated by this incalculable ocean. It soothed and made land-based tribulations infinitesimal.

Now the unfortunately land-locked Student must settle on the moldy reality of the *A plus B Hotel*.

He swept by his mailbox, ascended to his room anticipating rest prior to rehearsal. But no — he saw Davy Boy sitting at his door perusing various notes for him, perhaps rehearsing their dramatic interpretation. Student said goodbye to rest.

Davy Boy was absolutely shit-faced; the pressures of ongoing security issues for opening night caused him intense anxiety. He looked up at Student, acting out a soldier coming to attention.

"Ah, ha! Professor. Messages."

Struggling to his feet he lost balance — bounced off the door on the opposite side of the corridor, straightened and was preparing to read the first message when the disturbed occupant opened the violated door. He burned a hostile look at them both, then Davy Boy in particular.

"Hey, give me a break. That's my door, you drunken bastard."

The fellow wasn't a bad sort of neighbor, and Student was about to make amends but was preempted.

"KILL THE CAPITALIST COCKSUCKERS!!!"

Davy Boy wasn't the BTWG Sergeant At Arms for

nothing — his voice seemed sufficient to blow hinges off doors and windows. Like the infamous kookaburra bird, once an intoxicated Davy Boy was set off, he knew no volume control.

His neighbor slammed the door and there were a few shouted rejoinders here and there. These simply fired off Davy Boy's alarm system and he began shouting scurrilous slogans end on end. Student quickly opened his door and shoved Davy Boy inside slamming it shut — a bit ungracious, but it worked.

"It is OK, Davy Boy. Just give me the notes, and I'll read them. Sit down, sit down, right here."

"The sniveling bastards don't know what's in store for them after the revolution, Student."

The stalwart security specialist sat — thankfully subsiding. He removed a pint of rotgut vodka offering Student a brotherly pull that he declined. Davy Boy settled even more while Student scanned the messages. The most alarming of them was that Milly was down with the flu and would miss rehearsal.

Student's increasingly suspicious mind ran several dark scenarios past other than a flu bug. It was still three hours until rehearsal.

"Davy Boy, is O'Malley at the guild hall?"

"*Is O'Malley at the guild hall?*"

When drunk, he often repeated questions — giving him more time to think. He peered at the bedraggled wallpaper.

"No, Student. I don't think so. But he will be for rehearsals. A real trooper."

Student hurried Davy Boy out, urging him to return to the hall. An urgency drove him; he needed the Dart. Reaching the street he fast-walked to the garage, and checked his infamous vehicle out. Buses would not do. The attendant complimented.

"The most fucked up car in the joint, but my favorite."

He set out — oily smoke coiling from the exhaust, a post-cow pasture rattle keeping time to his pace. He picked and chose his way towards Milly's.

He parked the Dart smack in front of Milly's building beside an old-fashioned hexagon fire hydrant. He knocked on her door — this time a bit louder than usual while identifying himself. Student became suddenly aware O'Malley could be in there. He had not thought about that. No answer.

He knocked again — again identifying himself. Then through the door he heard her voice, despite the formidable battleship-grade iron plate of her portal.

"Student, I'm sorry. But I'm very sick. It's contagious."

"You alone in there?"

"I *beg* your pardon! Of course I'm alone."

That unseemly presumption just popped out — rather like a mouse spooked from its hole. Student instantly corrected course,

"I'm immune to flu. Don't worry. I just want to talk about the rehearsal tonight."

"Nobody is immune to the flu. And everyone depends on you to be well. Opening night is in nine days."

"Milly, open up; I'm a friend, not an enemy. Aren't I?"

There was a pause — Student wanted in, though the dread increased for what he might see.

"Yes, of course you are a friend."

"Then let me in."

There was a second pause — longer, and some movement — then the door unlatched. When Student eased around the door and closed it, the entire apartment was in near darkness, save for a night light over the entrance to the bathroom.

Since her space was a weird abode by any standards, this addition of Gothic lighting was downright medieval — a dungeon. Milly sat in her chair.

"I can't see anything. The lights are off."

"Student, I have let you in, but the lights will remain off. Isn't rehearsal soon?"

"I drove here. I want to see you, Milly. You don't have the flu, and O'Malley has beaten you up. Why protect someone like that."

"Because once I loved him; because once he was courageous in standing up to those who would pick on the poor and helpless. And prison ruined that person. You have not been to prison, Student; I have, both visiting and once for three months for trespassing. It changes you. Especially when you've done nothing wrong but express your own thoughts."

Student could hear that she was, though close to tears, clinging to her usual composure. What might he do? What should he do?

His father and mother always taught him to be gentle with things — with all living things, and surely humans. It seemed virtually automatic to follow this route.

Student peered through the darkness at the outline of this tall, lithe woman whose head was stuffed full of idealism and other mish-mashes most would consider poppycock. He had never seen a woman after a beating by a man. He hadn't an iota of preparation for this — especially with a close friend. Milly was all of that.

She looked down, keeping her face averted. He went over and though she straightened and held up a hand to ward him off, he gently lowered it with his left, and edged in next to her on the easy chair. Taking his index finger of his right hand he put it gently to her chin and turned her head until she faced him.

Her eyes looked up — and the weak ambient light in the doorway introduced Student to the grisly topic of beasts posing as men visiting violence on women. He knew what to do.

14.

Everything happened fast and Student wanted it that way. No one at the Butchertown Writer's Guild and Haywood Playhouse expected the scene which developed so rapidly: Everyone gawked in confusion seeing a new model of their heretofore sane, responsible director of *The Lower Depths* standing before them taking a combative stance before O'Malley.

"You swine! You have beaten Milly black and blue. It's time someone took you to task."

Simon Conners emerged from his office and despite great age moved towards Student fast. Davy Boy sat on a table corner, took a swipe at his eyes attempting to gather his wits. Simon made a calming gesture.

"Student. Ease off."

This was not the beginning of an act or scene, but real-time violence about to happen. Student was sober — this was not a wing ding — and he knew damned well what he was doing.

By God and galloping warthogs, he was in command here.

O'Malley was scrambling to seize the reality of Student's action.

"Now listen up! No Company members physically assault the other members on my watch. So O'Malley you are sacked from the play at once. You are a member of the guild, and I suppose have a right to be here. But if you are here I won't be. And above all, you stay far away from Milly. I **warn** you, O'Malley. Now when the play is over and you demand satisfaction, I will be available."

At well over six feet and 250 pounds O'Malley and Student's squaring off almost bordered on the comedic. However onlookers missed the humor, instead wondering if O'Malley would forthwith seize Student and snap his neck.

O'Malley allowed a thin smile — as he might when presented with a great sirloin steak.

"For starters, asshole, this is none of your business. And in case you haven't sense enough to notice it, you're available now."

Cast and guild members cried out in horror when O'Malley tossed out a feline-like stroke that ordinarily would have caught Student in his paw. But their outcries stopped when, fast as a terrier, Student bounded out of grasp, putting up a boxer's stance.

When O'Malley tried again, Student popped him with a left jab and right cross directly to his face and head.

"Now we've had enough of this shit! Back off. Both of you!" Simon stood fast between them, each hand holding an upward palm to the combatants. ". . . no fighting in the guild hall, fists or weapons."

O'Malley showed no signs of being hit save a red mark at the corner of his mouth. He appealed to Simon, an attempt at proletariat logic.

"He started it with his big mouth. I'm going to finish it."

"Baloney! He said when the play is over he'll give you satisfaction. Now the guild has invested everything in this play. Student is director and is doing a great job. He sacked you. That's within his prerogative. *Period*!"

O'Malley turned and walked towards the door; then stopped and pointed at Student, moving his index fingers back and forth.

"When this is over, I will definitely take you up on that offer, you little military toady. I'm going to make axle grease out of you"

He got gone, slamming the doors shut behind him. Student moved towards the stage, and two of the young ladies in the cast asked, "Student, where is poor Milly?"

"She was at the Emergency Hospital and now is home being taken care of. She says to continue without her. And we will."

Student allowed no time for the aftermath to develop a depressive mojo, and resumed minutes after O'Malley exited. Student called for the beginnings of rehearsal without further explanation or time for the cast to ruminate.

"Milly would want us to carry on, cast."

And it continued over the next few days — towards the premier night and grand opening of the BTWG Haywood Playhouse, Student Patterson residing director.

Student regretted nothing; if he was going to thrive in this business he must observe the oldest chestnut of them all was, *"The Show Must Go On."* He knew cast members were confused trying to decide if their director was a hero, a mad man, or in true dramatic fashion both.

If Student were a hero, his damsel in distress was not speaking to him. Milly had not designed her life with the concept of a gallant knight in the mix. She labored through each day wearing sunglasses and a hijab. This piece of exotic attire so impressed younger women in the company they too adopted them; hence, the female members of the company looked like members of an Islamic Thespian league.

It was strange to see a young woman wearing a hijab and flower-embossed Levi's, earth-core sandals exposing painted toenails.

Guild members hung back: Weirdness had arrived in their historic headquarters. What sort of socialist spin might they attach to the humiliation of their colleague and accomplished acolyte of Bomber Rothstein? Confusion reigned: For one BTWG member had been beaten by another and not just anyone, but a woman and Bomber Rothstein's youngest daughter. And most distressing — this action was done by an establishment-clad member of a U.S. reserve navy lieutenant. Davy Boy lamented this development.

"Student, did you have to do what you did in front of everyone? Now he'll kill you."

This quandary bothered him so much he sobered up. For atop this internecine outrage, there were outside events: The custom silk-screen posters advertising the opening night were being vandalized. Secondly the word was out that opening night attendees would be laced with *agent provocateurs* from right wing groups. The foremost of these was the John Birch Society's "Spitting Eagle Squadron," a militant arm of the lunatic outfit.

Davy Boy assembled a security plan for opening night while drinking end on end black coffees. His mind was filled with the one fear: *How might I avoid a donnybrook* — like the one that put the Haywood Playhouse out of business thirteen years before?

Jessica and Student managed only shorter times together, and he was careful to exclude any of the details of his recent professional outrage. Having O'Malley lurking in the wings every bit like walking home through a mine field.

Hiding the increased load on his nervous system was impossible to conceal from Jessica, as it might be from any intimate.

"Your love-making is off a bit, Student. Opening night jitters?"

They bided time in wonderful quiet and calm of her abode — it was Eden compared to his hotel. And this night was perfect stillness — the twins asleep down the hall. He and Jessica were both bathed in the soft overhead blue light. The entire boudoir was cast in this most discreet of lights — perfect for the purpose.

She sat Indian style next to him smoking a joint — something she did upon occasion, but never before sex. (*"Risks making it necessary for really getting off."*) He would take a hit now and then, but of late was doing nothing stronger than coffee, tea or breathing. Reality had to be competently wrestled with daily.

"I can't say I'm jittery; then again, I cannot deny it."

"God! You would make a perfect diplomat, you know that?"

"Can't say I've heard that before."

"Well, I spent my life around that. And, you would do fine."

Student secretly thought of taking his sword and running O'Malley through — making him the first Patterson murderer since an ancestor served as one of Oliver Cromwell's pike men. He thought to confess this black urge, but discussing one's inner potential of being a murderer made for lousy after-sex chat.

 Student reconsidered, why not take a hit off her joint? She lay next to him holding it to his lips, and then taking it away said,

"You know, I'm going to New York in June. I do have an uncle who is on my side — is on my daughters' side. My family are all on Long Island, but they own all sorts of real estate in New York — as in downtown. My uncle has a mammoth old studio for me, he says. In July — Godawful hot time, but it's cheap."

Her writing career she knew would be best served in New York City. Jessica wasn't the sort who passed up opportunities.

Student had never been to New York City nor could remember a desire to — or in fact, not to.

"Anyway, I really like you; you want to get into stage work, and New York is the place. The studio is smack dab in the middle of the theater district. There is no better locale, you know, to get started."

The cannabis rolled over him. Student recognized an extraordinary thing — Jessica was inviting him to New York with her — to share in a helluva future with powerful potential.

He never experienced someone desiring to share their future with him outside of Debbie.

"I didn't think you cared for me that much."

The seditious dope made him careless — he avoided being direct. But, it was the truth.

She bent over and looked him critically eye to eye — smiling.

"Soooooo, Jessica Dear goes on epic fucking sprees with men who she is just mildly attached to, is that it, Student?"

"Of course not. You have a terrible advantage on me — now I'm stoned. I like *you* a lot. There is that. But, I've begun sending out resumes and applications to various community playhouses and theaters advertising for assistant directors — a half dozen of them, actually."

"Community theaters? Like where?!"

"Seattle, San Diego, New Orleans — even back close to home in Des Moines. You know, all before I knew you'd offer me my big break."

She chuckled extinguished the joint and put the roach in an old tobacco can.

"None of those stacks up to New York. Anyway, in addition to me — my girls like you, You are the very first American to whom they desire to induct as an Ethiopian."

"Don't forget they will also make me a movie star."

She drew back a bit, appraised him as she might a bolt of cloth — then reached out and touched him on the forehead,

"*Got you!* Now, tell me who you have waiting in the wings, dear Student. You have somebody. And whoever it is, really taught you how to screw, if I may be so crass." She assumed a fortune tellers chant, "But — Herself sees it all! You're not free of them. Is this prophetess right, or no?"

He was paying the price of admission for the hit on the dope. His natural evasiveness was into the semi-wobbly stage. Had she planned this?

"Unless you've forgotten, you are the one who taught me about serious sex."

"Not a thorough denial."

Yet she desisted, perhaps resolving to precede her next fishing expedition with a bit more dope.

In the morning he pretended he had just arrived for breakfast, and the two girls lectured Student on how best to eat pop-tarts. He found in the little girls an edifying dimension to being just plain entertaining — confirming what he learned in directing children during the Christmas play.

This was an improvement over confronting reality which Student found a plague to a better life.

Like the entire cast, Milly was angered about the vandalized posters — silk screen originals by Eddy, both a cast member and long-time Butchertown Writer's Guild activist. They needed more in a hurry. Eddy got several volunteers that were cast members or friends of cast members; these jumped at the unique chance to work in the master's shop, an old warehouse down by the tidal seep.

Milly held up a defaced poster looking imploringly at Davy Boy, her voice became sad.

"Eddy does creative, superior posters — he is the labor socialists' Toulouse Lautrec. And here these horrible John Birch fascists destroy them with impunity."

Davy Boy collected the evidence.

"We'll catch them in the act and beat them to a pulp. Our newly loaned security squad enjoys that sort of thing."

He parted the curtains and was gone before Milly protested — like pointing out that pulverizing someone because they defaced an artful poster might be an overreaction. She stood before a set facade applying wallpaper.

Her dark glasses irritated Student. This is all he saw of her — for she had immediately begun a silencing regards Student after returning from the hospital. Student put his clipboard down and yielded to this anger.

"Milly, this silence is ridiculous. We're making the rest of the company very tense. I understand your views on what I did, but I don't agree with them. I was *not* out of control, and had a duty to everyone here. I thought we were friends — part of the solution and not the problem."

"You violated my right to privacy, employed violence ostensibly in my interests and utterly and forever insulted my independence as an emancipated socialist woman who acts upon her own interest without ownership by a man."

"Oh, for pity sakes! What good does ideological sloganeering do when faced with a brute like O'Malley? You accept his violence but not mine which was to prevent more? Jesus Christ, Milly you're fifty years of age and your head is in the clouds like a 15 year old."

"I *beg* your pardon, Student. I am 43. And my head is *not* in the clouds."

Student did mental footwork — she looked an easy decade more than that. Damn! He glanced self-consciously at the curtain; they had become loud.

He stepped closer to her — dark glasses hid eyes what he knew were alive with a fierce spirit.

Goddamn all dark glasses! His voice switched to *sotto voce*,

"Milly, I thought we worked through the petty gender differences between men and women early on?"

Student adhered to the gentlemanly policy of never referring to that week, yet he was close to being out of rhetorical ammunition — so hell, he violated this tenet. Her head jerked, and she reached up and removed the glasses. Her left eye — extending to the area over her nose — was now entering the yellow-blue phase.

"That is not fair, Student."

"Are we friends? Can we place this dispute on a cease-fire basis?"

"We are friends. And, yes I agree to a truce but without any intention of ceasing or modifying my views."

He extended a hand, and they shook on it.

Student didn't like this business — allowing one's emotions to wander drunkenly into the open. Human foibles were best shoved into a metaphorical barn somewhere, and the door barred securely behind them. Yes, surely.

At the security meeting in the BTWG office, most it was taken up spatially by the person of Constantine "Connie" Bolaslavsky, the president of the *Steam Brew, Stave Barrel and Glass Bottle and Jar Workers, International* commonly called in the old time labor movement the *Containers Union*. He was an ancient — the size of a Welsh bridge troll, save better dressed. Connie raised a hand the size of a coal scoop, pointing at the massive beam ceiling overhead.

"Ve take does John Borcher cogsuggeres and pound the fuck out of them. No bullshit on that, Simon. You guys help Container Union lotsa times with those fokking maggot packing companies — even trade. John Borchers? Hah! Means shit to us container guys. Ya, we get them and pound the fuck out of them."

Milly launched into a correction-of-goals, lecturing Connie they didn't need anyone hurt.

Davy Boy, Simon, Student and other attendees — did a good imitation of ignoring the futility of Milly's expectations when it came to the Containers Union. Connie took out a cigar, and looked suspiciously at Milly. He reached over, and with agility belying his great size plucked her glasses off; clearly, she'd known this giant for years.

"Hey, Milly honey, who did number on you; say who, and my guys kill the cogsugger. Cops? We don' give a shit. Touch you, and Connie's guys pound the piss outta whoever — goddamn. Bomber and I drank shit load of schnapps in our time. Bomber always on poor man's side. We owe your Pop major big time, honey."

Her fellow board members reacted as if kneed in the groin. She hurriedly took her glasses back.

"Just an accident, Connie."

Knowing Milly had been beaten was one thing — seeing was another; the three BTWG committee men closed their eyes, steeled themselves with a deep breath and stumbled on.

"OK, Connie. Even trade. You help us; we help you, and the assholes troublemakers will make themselves scarce. They know both you guys and us."

In the tradition of quiet diplomacy, Student had deftly acquired a security crew of a half dozen container union leviathans who happened to be free from jail that weekend. Davy Boy was no fool. Student began to have hopes opening night might not feature a major riot.

It was Wednesday night; opening was Friday night. Student left the security meeting and returned behind the curtains, and almost used a prop bed to flop on, but remembered its limitations. He was so tired he wondered if he could make it to the hotel.

Milly stopped him with an outstretched hand, and took him off a ways. She seemed contrite — maybe she was going to apologize for her less-than-grateful behavior; because of taking her side he faced single combat with a man nearly twice his size.

"Student, I feel very guilty — and I thought I should tell you. I have really thought about this. I was in the back sleeping three or four months ago — before that awful new year's event — the Chinese New Year's party. You came in here late to use the new pay phone; I woke up and heard everything, With your Aunt and parents. So, I know the pressure you were under. I'm not a snoop, it was an accident."

"No need. It was just my weekly call to Iowa."

"But you put your head down and beat your fist on the table — does that happen every week?"

Student for the moment soured,

"So, you were looking, too."

"I thought someone had died and was thinking of comforting you. I mean, whatever the details..."

And she trailed off, gazing down a moment — then finding resolve met him eye to eye, "... so, I've told you."

A suspicious demon slipped from his fatigued mind. Who else heard? Had she been back there working out issues between the genders with some other dupe. Well, whatever — she heard.

"Debbie. That is her name. And she didn't die. She was my fiancée. She dumped me when I was at sea. End of story. So. I'd better go; I'm so goddamned tired."

She set herself to one side and moved a hand to a hip,

"Now you're angry with me? I can hear it."

"No I'm not."

"You never curse unless you're peeved."

He turned and looked up patiently — he wondered if a dash of frankness might help get him home and some welcomed rest,

"Milly, since I began this business, you're the only friend I have. Of all those I could be angry with, you're the very last."

And he stepped forward, hugged her, then muttered a '*see you later*' and left, but before out of earshot, she answered,

"I'm so glad you said that, Student."

The suspicious demon was driven back to where it napped — or hibernated. One or the other. Or had it?

Student awoke fully aroused, yet sweating as if afflicted with swamp fever or mudflat ague. He was dreaming of Debbie, and that was something new. At no time in his life had he ever dreamed of her.

He was in a glen they discovered while in middle school, using it for their earliest body explorations, then for later heavy panting and dewiness. It was in an oxbow of Birch Creek. To reach their hideaway they waded upstream from Caster Bridge.

As they grew to high school age, he would watch her legs and buttocks as she navigated over the slick rocks leading the way to the copse, a perfect island in the middle of an ocean of corn and soy fields.

In this dream, Student arrived there first. An assignation? They were both of current age. She arrived without clothes there, but as she waded towards him he saw she had a black snake, nearly thick as her leg, entwined around her body. Emerging from the water, the snake slithered over to a tree, and once in it, Debbie was naked before him.

"I am your succubus, Stu. You have wanted me more than any other woman."

True enough: She seemed more voluptuous now; she looked to him, coming closer.

"I want you so far inside me each thrust will feel like forever.

Once you release it will be like the sky turning a wonderful pearl-white."

Great balls of fire! His middle turned to molten gold, and he became crazed to pour it into her. But when he stepped forward to take her, the snake opened its mouth and hissed, showing long, yellowed fangs that drooled amber, viscous venom.

'Fuck oh dear!'

Student bailed out of bed — rushed to the basin and dashed water over himself, and toweled off. He hated erotic dreams, and when they included snakes it didn't improve them. His subconscious had conspired with the evils of the night: He had graduated to having erotic dreams — to experience frustration *and* snakes *and* an unequivocal sexual Debbie.

He looked out his window — the fire escape had its usual crew of roosting pigeons jammed between the wall and the ladder. Lucky birds! It would be nice to scrunch down, remaining peaceful and safe through the night.

But if this was a succubus, it was the path to madness. Weren't dreams supposed be avenues of balm for unsettled minds?

His entire groin ached, and he inwardly wondered at the amount of sex he had partaken of late, versus the basic potential of his body to renew. Were, or as most women would say, *male people*, oversexed, under-brained toy poodles running around with little pink tongues and members hanging out?

Student made his way down the corridor, and descended to the streets two steps at a time. *'What the hell time is it'*, he wondered, and looking at the watch that replaced the one stolen saw it was a ridiculous four a.m. Even Big Lena's wouldn't be open until five.

But, Student would not risk sleep again with such things as a succubus running around in his dreamscape.

He heard a familiar voice — or, if not familiar, not strange. He took the alley exit out to the street, and there stood The Lecturer, as Student and a few others called him. His method for panhandling was unpopular on Market, and certainly north of Market, and he was confined to the south — and the farther south the better, as far as small businesses were concerned.

The Lecturer would plant a sign reading, *"Authoritative Lectures 25 Cents,"* a coffee can for tuition. He would then work into a rant on one topic or another — some semi-gibberish, some not — and keep going until he collected enough, or was just chased off. The Lecturer, like Davy Boy in his cups, required no amplification.

But here he was at 4:00 a.m., lecturing to nobody. Student had seen pedestrian audiences of one or two passersby a minute. But none a minute, or even per half hour, was a new low.

"THERE IS A GREAT STORM CLOUD GATHERING THAT WILL SWEEP AWAY ALL THOSE WHO WILL NOT YIELD TO THE NECESSITY OF EATING WHOLE WHEAT PRODUCTS."

Student tried to remember if The Lecturer featured nutritional topics before, but no matter — at least he was making sense. He passed by, then felt guilty since it wasn't bad advice — crossed over and put 50 cents in the tin can.

He turned away, and was just taking the corner to the BTWG hall when The Lecturer segued to the efficacy of boiling water before drinking it.

Student took the key from his pocket, then noticed the lock was undone. Through the window he could see a light; he looked around through the street-level windows. He saw no one, and along the curb there were no cars. He supposed it could be Simon, or even Davy Boy — or Milly for that matter. Time was growing close to opening night — just somewhat more than 24 hours.

Everybody was getting strange. Hell, he certainly was!

When he closed the double door behind him, he called out, but there was no response. Then,

"Well folks, looks who's here!"

He swiveled to see O'Malley step before him; his coat was off, and he moved between the door and him to intercept in the event he bolted. Student thought *'Oh, shit!'* but managed an even tone,

"The agreement was, I would give you satisfaction after opening night, and you were to stay away from here. In fact, they said you went to L.A."

"I came back. And, I'm shipping out tonight. So, I'm changing our schedule a bit. Looks like we'll both miss opening night."

He caught Student on a rapid lunge forward, peeled him off his feet and tossed him up against the wall. There would be no boxing match tonight. Student had the same statistical chances of successfully fighting O'Malley as he might a forklift. Struggling for breath, he tried to maintain a dialogue.

"O'Malley, we are both for the working man and woman — I'm on your side. "

"Save it."

He pulled Student away from the wall, then slammed him against it again — tearing his shirt and jacket — knocking him breathless and senseless.

"Hey, what are you doing to him?"

The voice of The Lecturer caused O'Malley to move away from the wall; Student's vision hadn't cleared, but he knew the voice.

O'Malley managed an unbrotherly snarl, "Get the fuck out of here you crazy bastard."

"Oh, come on! You have a john in here? I can piss anywhere, but I need to poop."

"I said to get gone!"

"There's one in back of the office, to the right. Go ahead."

Student found voice and sense at the moment his vision cleared; The Lecturer nodded and headed towards the facility. O'Malley was caught off-balance and lost focus.

He took one hand away from Student perhaps to gesture '*outside*' to the Lecturer, and a single paw restrained Student: It had to be now.

Student rifled forward, using the wall as a springboard, and butted O'Malley in his chest — putting all his 165 pounds behind it, and it worked — his assailant tumbled back, in fact putting out his other hand to stop himself from going on his backside when he caught himself on the corner of the table.

Student shot off à la an Olympic sprinter at the gun. He swerved around O'Malley's gorilla-length arm who moved at once between the door and himself. Student had not gone for the door nor did he jump up on the stage fleeing behind the curtains. He took a third, unexpected route: He disappeared into the sultry shadows behind the playhouse — a cavernous no-man's-land comprising the old interior of the basement warehouse where years ago kegs of beer had been stored.

He had elected a blind alley, and O'Malley knew it.

Student had a single idea stemming from his tour of the area with the fire marshal: He located the closest of the half dozen old fire stations in those shadows, pulled on the handle of the case holding the fire ax but it held solid. Dozens of old grade 'B' action flicks manifested themselves in an instant. He reared back and kicked out the glass, reached through and grabbed this heinous object-of-war. It was painted red, with an ugly head sporting a blade on the right side, and a butt and spike on the other.

The two men met each other on the zone where the light met the dark of the old warehouse section. O'Malley stopped so fast, he came up on the balls of his feet.

"Now what, O'Malley? Will I miss opening night now?"

Student slunk down in a Saxon stoop — inching forward — holding his weapon in classic style: One hand a foot below the top, and another at the junction of iron and oak. A flow of blood from a flesh wound ran down his arm completed a grisly scene indeed. Only a Roman triple-layered ox shield, or a less historic pistol or shotgun would function against this unholy weapon.

O'Malley's great size now only functioned as an inviting target for the 10-pound head of what was more of a pole-ax than an ax.

O'Malley's eyes moved everywhere, but always came back to the ax; since a table had been knocked outwards, his hind end came against it — stopping him. He edged around it, keeping his eyes on the weighty head of the weapon.

"Student, I was just going to rough you up a bit — hell, you made me look like a bum in front of everyone."

"Sit down on the floor."

"What!? And have you behead me? Fuck you, I'll take my chances standing up."

A toilet flushed, and their life and death scene went into a stop motion when The Lecturer emerged glancing at both of them.

"Did you guys know you're out of toilet paper? I had to use paper towels."

The Lecturer took a few extra seconds to appraise the strange tableaux and offered,

"Remember, all of us have our good and bad sides."

And walked up the stairs and was gone. O'Malley held his

hand out, was about to add something mollifying when Student brought the ax down upon the table between them smashing it — sending pieces of laminate and wood spraying all over, O'Malley put his hand up to his face to shield it.

"I *said* sit. I'm so utterly angry and scared shitless I should *kill* you!"

The manner which Student used the awful weapon indicated background with using a fire ax. O'Malley sat, first on a chair.

"No, on the floor."

And did so.

Student kicked debris out of the way, took out coins from his pocket and went to the pay phone.

"Now I'm going to do what I should have when you beat hell out of Milly — call the cops."

O'Malley looked patiently at the ceiling — as if dealing with a difficult assistant.

"I have no weapon; you have the ax, and I just came from Milly's and she forgave me several times over."

"You what?! Did you beat her again?!"

"No, just the opposite."

There was a sly smile and he raised a finger and pointed to the phone,

"Go ahead, call her. She'll vouch for me."

Student could not conceive of such a thing; furthermore, if O'Malley had gone there, she would have called him — or somehow warned him of his return from L.A.

"I promised I wouldn't harm you Student. Plus I'm about to ship out, and didn't expect to see you here at — what is it? — four in the morning."

"You *promised* her! She believed you!"

"Of course she did. Student, you dimwit, you have a lot to learn about women: Once a man finds the right combination between her sweet spot and the rough stuff a woman is your back door mare forever. My problem lately, is I went a bit too far. Won't do that again."

Student's hands froze on the ax handle and the coins — the entirety of it overwhelmed. He quickly took fresh resolve; what difference did it all make?! The bastard was going to kill him.

"I'm still calling. I'll not have you lurking behind every corner. And I'm telling them I have evidence of you being behind bombing the Federal car in front of the building."

"You what!!"

Student put a dime in and dialed "0". Before the operator came on, he offered,

"O'Malley, I would say that you are screwed."

And Student completed the call.

Dress rehearsal was Thursday night, and it went poorly. Everyone was jittery, plus word got out that O'Malley had showed up and there was a bitter scene. Student described it only as ". . . *some trouble,*" but assured all that O'Malley had shipped out to Palau at 5:30 that morning.

Questions persisted about blood stains and broken glass on the floor, a table bashed in two — all linked suspiciously with a fire ax leaning against one of the massive support beams. It was not one of the properties for *The Lower Depths*. The only explanation Student would offer was, *"It got a bit tense for a few minutes, is all."*

There was, once again, a pall of dark between Student and Milly, and this time it was she who wondered at its origins. She did not have opportunity to question Student, for he and everyone had dress rehearsal where she spent most her time in the prompter's box — a lonely station.

Student had difficulties looking at her, his mind was shaken by O'Malley's words. The dressing on his arm only belied his lighthearted version of events. All guessed there had been some form of carnage.

Perhaps it was this ambiance that pushed the rehearsal into the red.

The cast stepped all over each other, save for Sterling who was indeed a phenomena. All were sure they were privy to seeing a true theatrical talent in its infancy — nothing seemed to rattle Sterling.

Student's biggest job was the cast meeting after rehearsal. As everyone went through their check lists and talked the errors and weak spots out. Milly, then Student came in with positive reinforcement for the following night,

"It is not uncommon for a new company such as we are to have a rough time on the first dress rehearsals." Student allowed a reassuring smile, and opened both arms in a *voila* gesture, "*You see, that is why they call them dress rehearsals!*"

He hugged who needed hugging mixed in with telling them tomorrow night at around 10:30 p.m., it would be a matter of theatrical history. He announced the time and place of the cast party afterwards, (Big Lena's All Star Café). They then thinned out, going home in ones and twos.

It was time for a belated narration of the early morning impromptu theatrics.

Simon Conners, Davy Boy and a few other guild members hung close by. None knew much about this morning's set-to with O'Malley. Milly sat, her large dark eyes held down, his account had nothing for her but sadness. Student harbored anger towards her; he cared less for her sadness than his near-encounter with mayhem.

He told the account straight, no added color. It didn't need it.

Simon and Davy Boy listened without sign of alarm until he got to the police being called. Cops were an anathema, he imagined, to socialist-activists. Student continued anyway, sour looks aside,

"He was lucky to get a couple of lazy cops — they made O'Malley agree that if they took him to his ship he would get on it. And once on it, he had better stay on it."

"Jesus Christ, Student. Did you have to call the cops! He might have ended up serving the rest of his term in the Federal pen. I think that's six years."

"Davy Boy, he was going to maim or kill me — as it is, my entire torso is bruised. I have a nasty wound on my arm. Sorry to sound insensitive, but he could serve twice six years, and I just don't care."

Simon loaded up his pipe, puffed away until it got going,

"Actually, Davy Boy, events might have been a helluva lot worse. We could have body parts laying around here."

They all took in his assessment, and Milly suddenly sat up straight, dazed.

"I cannot believe it is the same man."

Student didn't want to humiliate Milly but he could not stop resentfulness creeping in.

"I know he said he wouldn't harm me, Milly. I just wish you would have given me a heads up, Milly. Something."

She came to life — stood up, shaking her head as if a live bee or wasp flew into her hair.

"What are you talking about?!"

"You didn't see him yesterday?!"

"No! Did he tell you that?"

"Just a minute, this ugliness has gone far enough. It is dividing us."

Simon spoke in the imperative; his voice brought immediate

silence. He pointed his pipe to both of them — then Davy Boy.

"You're talking about a ruined man who was mentally fricasseed by years in a Federal pen. Forget him. He's gone in more ways than one. You've both got a play."

Milly turned and disappeared behind the curtains.

Student and all looked to each other with bovine haplessness.

Steeling himself for a crisis of confidence Student stepped up to the stage. He slipped through the curtains and there was Milly, putting on her street shoes. She looked sadly at Student. She kept her voice low.

"Student, I don't know precisely what he said — but do you think I would put you in terrible danger. You *believed* him."

"I was never so scared in all my life, Milly. "

He sat next to her, worked his arm around her waist and they leaned against each other, staring ahead at their reconstruction of a 1900 Russian flophouse. Neither of them said anything, for when a solid truth is said, there is nothing more.

It was in the slender hours of the early morning that he woke up beside Jessica and stole out to the kitchen for a drink of something.

When they picked him up that evening he had decompressed as Jessica rewarded the girls for being "good sorts" with a slow ride, including commentary, up through Chinatown.

As usual Student found Jessica and the twins a balm. He constructed a fantastic cover story about his injuries — that he slipped on his fire escape while escaping the clutches of a hideous spider in his room. Having seen the exterior of the *A plus B Hotel* the twins lectured him on his choice of facilities.

This began the decompression.

For now, it was important to him for the twins to enjoy

themselves and feel positive about the world; surely, better hotels came without such spiders; did not life hold out finer things?

Later he would tell Jessica the grimmer truth, which did not hold out finer things, at least not necessarily.

Taking part in the experience of the girls, getting on with Jessica — and directing the play — was his first contact with an emotionally assertive life.

Why didn't Patterson men follow this path? His father, wonderful soul, sought the self-sustaining chicken farm. He could have years ago gone into big-time chicken production by cranking out scrawny broilers and watery eggs for supermarkets at a faster pace.

He listened to naysayers, even his own daughter's clod of a husband, about the poor choices he made. And instead of grabbing a gravy boat and nailing the greedy bastard over his cranium the senior Patterson politely ate dinner and suffered through it. Until Student took O'Malley to task, he followed his father's lead and kept such expressions of justice wrapped tightly, save for his disastrous descent into drunken sprees.

Oh yes! There was that.

Better to have kept sober, and showed up at such social eyesore as the Chinese New Year's party, freed the rooster, get up on a chair and shout,

"You are all avaricious human monstrosities and would serve mankind best by finding a private corner and slitting your throats."

Student found himself getting angry. *'Control yourself, Student, for God's sakes. You can't change the past, you poor sap."*

He opened some orange juice, sat and poured himself a glass, looking into it he wondered if it actually came from an orange.

'That's the problem with being raised on a farm, you always wonder about that stuff', and began to feel increasingly sorry for himself.

His mind returned without warning to the early yesterday morning. Student resented being forced to the use of deadly weapons to save himself.

He looked forward returning to his comfortably benign home in the summer, though he wondered after the situation there.

Yes, he would leave San Francisco soon. Getting distant as possible from the Jenkins, a Ph.D. program or in fact the BTWG couldn't come too early for Student.

"Mr. Student, may we have juice too?"

Both girls stood in the kitchen entry. They were wrapped together in one blanket, heads protruding like a two headed raccoon.

"Girls, you began the night in pajamas, where are they?"

They reversed — went back, got their pajamas on, and returned.

"Why did you take your pajamas off?"

He again was suckered into an entirely tangential topic. He poured them each a small glass of juice, listening to their logical explanation. Then Mother appeared, just somewhat more covered than her daughters,

"What do we have here? Now they'll pee their beds?"

"They were telling me why they take their pajamas off and it is quite interesting — something to do with not wrinkling them."

Jessica relieved them of the remainder of both their juices, and herded them back, leaving Student to remember that opening night was just twelve hours off.

They then sat together; she lay on her outstretched arms, and looked at him patiently, with an edge of coyness.

"Are opening nights always preceded by deadly combat?"

"Truthfully, I look forward returning to Iowa where if I had good sense, I would send my parents off to Florida and raise chickens for the remainder of my life."

She raised a hand, and placed the pad of her index finger directly in the middle of his forehead, as if pressing an elevator button.

"What, or who, has you Student — or a part of you? See, I'm pressing your activate button, and you *must* tell me, because I know it is not me."

An ancient instinct urged him to silence, regards discussing one *known* woman to those previous. He had told Milly because she had overheard, so informing her was a mere clarification.

He had a new idea.

"Who says you don't have me? Also, why don't you speculate, Jessica? You're the writer — you are creating characters. You certainly know me."

"Fair enough," she sat up and closed her eyes. "It is a *She*, of course. *She* is back in Iowa; *She* needs rescuing from disaster by her childhood *amore*."

Student was at once impressed, but in the next few seconds suspicious. Too close.

"That was pretty damned good, Jessica."

"Thank you. Instincts. I have good writer's instincts. I feel things from people."

Later, in the unequaled peace following lovemaking, Student looked at his partner through heavily lidded eyes and admitted that even in the depths of sleep, Jessica looked suspicious. He concluded her guess could be general enough to be based on observations, then again . . .

It was strange. She was strange; her daughters even stranger.

He had begun the cruise on the "Bugly" almost twenty

months before — bound for normalcy. His fiancé was mentally on board with him — planning such things as Dutch Doors and patios with all-weather outdoor furniture.

The Gods had reached out and snatched him from this peaceful path. They were uncaring that way. Perhaps they did this as a form of entertainment.

The Haywood Playhouse filled gradually to a full house. Davy Boy and his quartet of goons from the Containers' Union wore matching red jackets to signify their office. Their dignity factor was hampered because the goons' coats were somewhat small and poorly concealed the ¾'s size Louisville Sluggers beneath. They looked forward to dragging John Birchers, or other troublemakers, into the back-reaches of the cavernous warehouse and suggesting different entertainment for the evening.

Other BTWG members under the direction of President Emeritus Conners, managed seating with two of Big Lena's waitresses selling and collecting tickets. Big Lena lured them in by telling them the play was a romance. The former circus pro was in charge of makeup — having at one time been a dresser for world-famous clowns.

The planning was professional, and Student —like the busiest hockey goalie on record, skated from task to task, and crisis to crisis. Their excitement was simple:

Student and the entire cast were like children setting up a first time lemonade stand, only to discover that everyone wanted to buy lemonade.

The house was filling, and the buzz of the audience was ominous — frightfully audible on the other side of the curtain. Milly began to pass along reassuring hugs to diverse cast members, relentlessly creating a lifeline of morale support.

Sterling — their lead — though young, was a wonderful model — as always, he was steady-at-the-helm.

An hour before curtain, Student went outside the hall and waited for Jessica who showed with the Simca; she had come dressed in her "I.Magnin" employee garb, and was stunning. No one in the cast, or indeed the BTWG had seen her before, or indeed knew outright Student had a girlfriend. She turned heads everywhere as he led her in, and they took their seat on a slightly elevated portion — off by itself — a concession to his director's status insisted upon by the seating department.

"Do you think they'll be a riot, Student?"

Jessica asked this while perusing the program, which included a woodcut of Gorky on the cover.

"It is not a word we use here."

"Good, I already pulled you out of one."

Just then Davy Boy's goons sniffed out two FBI agents, and there was a great shoving match and I.D. showing. Simon at once interceded. Student reached the crisis point next. Davy Boy did not care about affiliation.

"They're armed."

The goons knew that qualified them as troublemakers, and instinct caused them to reach beneath coats and grip their bats.

"For Christ sakes, guys, they're on duty, and they're welcome."

"Ya, back off you guys. They're Feds. They're always buzzing around here."

With his gravitas Simon set everything to rights but the Feds were angry, and insisted on checking the goons for firearms, but all they found were baseball bats. There was a logical explanation for them.

"We're going to batting practice afterward and want to get the feel of them."

The goons all had a great laugh and the agents filtered into the crowd to make notes on un-American activities and of radical sorts recognizable to them. Within a few minutes, this included Jenkins and a young woman decked out in the finest mod attire available — no secondhand store for her. Jenkins wore a Nehru jacket and natural-stone love beads, his pricey alligator shoes rather clashed with the beads.

"This is my niece." He slapped Student on the back, congratulating him on the full house, his eyes feeding greedily on Jessica, who greeted his niece with what he knew was her ironic smile. It seemed they had been in the same creative writing course.

At that point Milly approached with a backstage problem. Jenkins held his arms out,

"Why look here. The beauty of the Butchertown Writer's Guild — you must be ecstatic over this show of support."

She mumbled an acknowledgment. Student knew by the look of her she had other pressing business. Excusing himself he followed her backstage joining Simon and Davy Boy looking over two count sheets, the latter looked heavenward for help.

"Student, there's 118 here; we've let in 18 more than fire code allows. Those goddamned gorillas miscounted on me."

They looked closely at the two scratch sheets, and Simon nodded.

"Yup. Jesus, we could be closed down here — you know, if the bad guys knew of this. All they need do is call the fire department."

The premises were Simon's call, but the work and dedication were the cast's, and Student represented the cast, who appealed to Simon.

"We could let it roll — curtains in 14 minutes Hell, we *have* to."

They agreed. The huddle broke and Simon reminded Davy Boy to let no one else in — they were 'sold out'.

Student went back behind the curtains, found a worried Milly — she knew well the sword of Damocles hung over their entire effort.

"Milly, the Gods are with us", and hugged her a good long one, broke, looked her up and down, nodding.

"You look ready for the swells on the east end," She was dressed in her best — a long black dress that just touched the floor, with red shoes sticking out — a long way out, her feet being notoriously long.

When Student rejoined Jessica on his "conductor's platform," Jessica watched with poorly concealed mirth as Jenkins and his niece took their seats.

"She's married and she's not his niece."

"Well, he's married and he's not her uncle."

The lights went down halfway, and Milly came out. She was flawless before a crowd — certainly, she'd done this before. The temptation for political zealots when they have a captive audience is to go wild with 'cause' rhetoric. She did not.

After welcoming all she gave a short historic context of the play and why it was the BTWG's choice to re-open the playhouse.

And that was it. Damn! Student was proud of her

After applause for her introduction, the lights went all the way down, the curtains opened, and by God and Maxim Gorky, the play began.

Jessica took Student's hand; he wrapped his arm around her waist — they braced as two people about to embark on a roller coaster ride of unknown construct.

The earliest critique of the play was when one of the four security gorillas from the Container's Union (all four stayed through the performance, another good sign) came to Student after the numerous curtain calls, and said, *"You know, Captain, that's a pretty goddamned good play."*

Sterling accepted the two dozen roses from the audience for the cast, and Student had no idea who thought of that — he'd been concerned other vegetable matter might come from the audience rather than roses.

Student could not recall feeling as exultant he did the moment the final curtain went down. The reason was simple. There *had* been no other moment like it. Disbelief blended with unbridled pride and Student knew that he wanted to do this for always — or the foreseeable future, and he needed to get far better and more experienced. Tonight he was lucky; he wouldn't always have Milly around.

Words of congratulations were strewn about him — glorious confetti at a party! Student did not know if Jessica was holding his arm or holding him up.

A short, elderly lady threaded her way through the praise-givers and taking his arm, put a card in it, stepping up on tip-toe to be heard. Her words were clear with an accent unmistakably Slavic.

"You did a good job with a hard play, Mr. Patterson. Here's my card. My name is Gulashka, Ulovna Gulashka. Seattle Hearthside Players, you wrote us. Can I breakfast with you tomorrow at the Jack Tar Hotel?"

He thanked her and shook her hand before she receded away. He moved towards the back of the stage with Jessica following. Patrons were leaving, though a few were lingering inside the door in animated discussions. He saw Simon and Davy Boy taking a heavy hit from the former's flask.

Back stage, the cast was falling over itself — Sterling was breaking up the bouquet of roses and giving them to each player. He and Milly caught site of one another, and she was — finally, after all these weeks — smiling, laughing and when he caught hold of her, despite both their wounds, Student lifted her up, elevating her as high as his strength would allow, announcing,

"Three Cheers for our Stage Manager and Guiding Light!"

And they did — more than that.

Then, two by two, or in larger clumps, they made their way towards the cast party at Big Lena's All Star Café, which tonight Student knew the most aptly named eating establishment in San Francisco. No doubts at all.

On their way to the cast party Jessica instead diverted to her Simca, saying she was very tired and would head home.

"I've a big political reception tomorrow, and set up starts in late morning. Big money though."

She had become uncharacteristically morose. He knew her capacity for work and play, and it was nowhere close to spent. She was angry.

"No! Come to the cast party, and then — we'll don't you want to help me celebrate this victory properly?"

"No. I don't. It wasn't my victory. In fact, I felt like a prop."

They had never argued and Student didn't want to sully this evening with starting now. Still, her anger didn't make any sense yet instinct told him, *'Don't push her.'* They walked to the Simca, she got in, pecked him on the cheek and drove the unlikely contraption off through Butchertown, and north towards Market and beyond.

Student breathed deeply to steady himself — his own anger found the smallest of vents despite the great success of the evening. He guessed his jubilation with Milly aroused jealousy in Jessica, and he never perceived Jessica as jealous. Confident people were not usually jealous, and Jessica was all confidence. No, it must be something else.

Major news at Big Lena's during the after-performance blowout was that Sterling was offered an on-the-spot four year scholarship to the Yale School of Drama. Keeping attention to rumors, someone from the school — or their representative — heard of the young talent before that night's performance.

"Are you going to go?"

And Sterling acknowledged to one after the other, he would, but only if Big Lena would accompany him as his makeup person.

No one needed more fuel for this exuberance; hence, Student held out telling anyone about Ulovna Gulashka. For a well-known figure in theater such as her — his good fortune seemed hardly believable. Best wait for their meeting, maybe she needed janitorial help. All he'd done was one children's Christmas play and tonight's one-time performance.

No one had discussed other performances, assuming they would be lucky to get one performance behind them without being driven into the streets by angry theater goers.

Simon voiced news to the contrary.

"Do two more next weekend; one on Friday, another on Saturday. We made five hundred dollars tonight! First time we've done that with a function."

Student — everyone — agreed at once to it — the Saturday run being the performers gate, where they would get all the ticket receipts.

"I just think that is fair; actors are workers too."

Milly talked this up, for making a little side money pleased everyone. And why not?

Student excused himself early with the reason he was utterly fatigued. It was a hybrid of truth and to just get off by himself. Milly cornered him, and congratulated Student again, adding,

"It is too bad your lady friend left early. She looks so stunning, Student. Jessica is her name?"

"Yes. A writer."

She probably wanted to ask more questions, but thankfully did not. He slipped out onto the dreary streets of Butchertown. Taking the first corner, he saw a couple of denizens hanging out in the receding doorway of a shuttered bakery.

A civic minded sort had scrolled *"No Pissing"* inside the window, and someone responded *"Fuck you"* on the outside — a sort-of absented dialogue of diverse views.

Student reminded himself that every night was a performance of *The Lower Depths* in Butchers' Town. The dilapidated section of the city needed no stage drama to establish that. He paused to stare into another empty shop — with the words "Harry's Electric Motors" still readable across the window.

He wondered, *'Where is Harry now'?* It was a dreary issue.

Student's flush of victory and joy was subdued by the time he ascended the stairs. When he reached the landing at the third floor he came eye to eye with a fist-sized brass padlock and matching hasp on his neighbor's door. This wad of hardware sealed room 102 for the requisite fourteen days when all contents would be sold for back rent. The more positive outcome was the resident coughing up back rent to Edwin Fong, _Resident Manager_.

Entering his room, feelings of exuberance were now drained. He especially became aware he would occupy his bed alone — for the first time in many nights. Better this way tonight.

He had the same feeling when coming off late night-watch

aboard the *Bugly:* He was proud of commanding an entire naval vessel as OD through a watch and felt an urge to tell someone. But instead he would enter his 'stateroom' to be greeted by Ensign Fremont in the top bunk sleeping head under his pillow with his butt humped upwards. Often the wretched man would be muttering unintelligibly, lost in some dreadful dreamscape.

In the tiny abode's night light, the poor devil's "Yale" pennant — the only icon of his school days — was sole occupant of the bulkhead. Student would squeeze into his bunk, and locating the only good position settle in.

He would hear and feel the plodding *"Bugly"* lifting and settling in the seas — the distant sounds of machinery beneath. The rhythm of it, always the overwhelming rhythm — and he would drift off into sleep often wishing someone might whisper in his ear, *"Good work, Student. Good work."*

15.

In the morning after he breakfasted with Ulovna Gulashka he gathered together enough quarters to play a row of slot machines and called Iowa. He was loaded with breaking news of the successful opening and the job he'd accepted in Seattle. And not least of all, meeting Ulovna Gulashka, who at 75 still retained a semblance of the beauty she showed on the silent screen in Russia.

"She was in American movies after the war; she played the housekeeper in *Abbot and Costello South of the Border.* She'd been in Mexico for 10 years at that point teaching theater at the National Academy."

But his parents were more impressed in him, his success and that of his cast. They knew he was close to the cast — in fact, his letters always contained interesting character sketches of one or another.

The quarters slid down the gullet of the pay phone. He and his parents had to cover a lot. Since the job would not begin until September first he insisted on coming home and helping them pack up and move to southward.

Close to the end of the quarters, his mother who invariably ran "cloaked" about Debbie, broke radio silence, initially with another matter,

"Your Aunt thinks you're mad at her. You don't call much, nor write."

The three knew it was certainly not this, for he loved his aunt almost as much as his mother.

"I *do* write. But calling is problematical with," but he broke off his thought; it needn't be said.

"Well, Student," his father came out with it. "Debbie and her baby have gone over to her uncle Gene's place; he's provided a cottage there, and she has a car, and is going it alone. The whole family is still in an uproar and sides have been taken. But Debbie has become very independent, and stays out of it."

He said nothing, save he would call Aunt Lila more frequently. After they made their farewells and signed off, the news about Debbie made him feel easier. Returning home was always a bright spot, and if Debbie had remained with Aunt Lila visits would be complicated.

Might it be wise if Student never saw her again? This could be easily done, for at the beginning of the school year she would be in Maine. But they had so much background, he should visit to at least begin a friendship. He did not see her as an enemy.

Debbie's uncle's place was only two or three miles off from his parents — he was her mother's brother. But like all Debbie's people, her uncle thought Student's father was crazy and worse a Methodist who voted Democrat. Now the Pattersons would be further demonized having taken in Debbie. It was a welcome relief to Student to be shut of those two family lines of historical primitives.

He did not take a bus all the way to Jessica's, but instead got off halfway again and walked the remainder. He wanted to think — here seemed to be never enough time to just think.

Student wandered up one hill, then down another — stalling. He was like the geese his mother used to keep who sensed more than knew. Student felt trouble awaited at Jessica's, and struggled to fit the now of it into some order of cause and effect.

In all the permutations of the situation, the only satisfactory one was, she had asked him to share her life in New York City, the heartbeat of American theater life, and he turned it aside.

Now with the Ulovna deal, it would surely be out.

"I don't want to go to New York."

"Well, don't then, especially looking like that."

His solo declaration was not solo; a woman stood cleaning the window of a tiny boutique clothing store — she looked him up and down.

"Nothing personal, of course."

He smiled, veered away and gave himself a demerit for talking to himself, and corrected to a course directly for Jessica's. Best to get on with it other than making a gibbering fool of himself. There would be no escaping the issue now.

Student vainly hoped she would be in a better mood as he might be winning the Irish Sweepstakes.

She let him in but was getting ready to leave. "I'm having lunch with a friend. I have time for a cup of coffee, though." Her face was tight; her eyes looked at him, a glint of challenge to them.

For now, he would take what she gave. He sat.

"How did your breakfast go with the Russian — who was she."

"Ulovna Gulashka. New Director of the Seattle Hearthside Players; she offered me the job as her assistant, and I took it. It begins September first, and I will be going back to Iowa soon to help my parents move to Florida — get some joy in their life, away from those winters."

She watched the brewer burp away — it took eons. In the manner of eighteenth century British navy terminology, Jessica had dropped the gun doors open and had rolled the guns outboard, ready to fire. *Jesus,* he thought, . . . *this might get ugly.*

Jessica was a tough little thing, and thought nothing of

kicking any guy's hind end who groped her at any of the dozens of gatherings she helped cater.

Moving her gaze to him, she leaned forward over the table and put an index finger on the tabletop, keeping time with her words,

"It is like this: After I got back from Ethiopia, the only good thing any man has told me, is I'm built for fucking. So, I'm forced to provide my own cheering section. *I'm going* to New York City; *I'm going* to be a kick-ass writer of novels. *I'm going* to dress foxy and put in appearances at literary gatherings my agent says are best. And soon the girls and I are never going to be dependent on relatives again. *This* is how it will be, Student."

"I admire that. And, I have never said or thought anything to the contrary, so count me out from others, thank you."

"Problem is, you never say much at all."

As she poured coffee, he noticed that her hand was just a tad unsteady; her ears were still a long ways back, her litany of "I'm going's" had not vented enough heat. Some remained.

"Jessica, why are you so angry with me?"

"Student, you never take your current piece of ass and introduce her to your previous piece of ass. It is bad form."

Her chin was out — and now Student felt *his* back go up:

In this metaphysical boxing match, their corner people had pulled out the stools and fled the ring. The bell had sounded.

The two mentally circled, Student knew he had the advantage — he was better than she at concealing an outer show of temper,

"Milly is my associate and friend; I couldn't have done the job I did if it weren't for her."

"You've had sex with her, and not that long ago. Jesus Christ, Student, women know that right away, you dumb shit."

"And I know *you've* read my mail, for that was no guess the other day — too close."

She wheeled — thrusting a finger at him.

"And I'm a better woman for it. I'm giving myself to you — I don't know how many times a week, almost knocked me up — then sharing my kids with you, and you tell me nothing. So yes! I read several of them. Debbie has you by the balls."

"That is an outrage! I trusted you and for sure Debbie doesn't have me by any point of my anatomy."

This was a terrible first: Voices had risen; but in a moment of otherworld intervention, a peculiar vapor of pacification closed over them. Their own words returned to them — echoes, as if they were from someone else as if they were listening to a poor radio play.

She slumped and took a clip from her hair and tossed it on the counter. He did not expect tears from someone who at age 22 watched a firing squad march her husband and father of her kids out the front entrance of their house and kill him in the street.

Student had been saved by her from an inferno fed with pints of cognac at risk to herself. And without doubt, they had made wonderful love dozens of times everywhere. And the most beautiful thing, Jessica had daughters who wanted to take him to Ethiopia and make him a star.

He was leaving; she was too. Thousands of miles were ahead to different worlds. Was it a sadistic truth that for humans all good things had to cease?

She took him by his hand, and rising pulled him along while moving towards the stairs. Student assumed either she did not have a lunch date, or decided to skip it.

16.

Seers of Future Present

(Dressed as Lumberjacks complete with logging boots)

Student now is the moment for you to get cracking and be a really good guy. Look at the alternatives! You occupy a top position on the hit list of those females of ruthless justice — the Eumenides, those harpies of Fate. Take our fair warning, and watch your posterior around them, Student.

But Good News!! You have been given a reprieve, probably due to our hard work. We assured them you are a fine fellow as long as you lay off the cognac.

The Fates have shown mercy by granting their gentler daughter, Destiny, to take positive charge of your case, and now you have a clear horizon off the starboard quarter. Destiny has opened up a rich benefice of great theatrical achievements. The fact remains you double crossed Debbie, and Destiny has agreed to overlook that — and advises you to walk away from what is old history — last week's news.

You know well the true path of goodness. However, if you cross the Ancient Fates in this all important matter, and disappoint Destiny? All we can say is, better you than

**us. And as a final benefit of our near perfect
vision, let us warn you away from taking that
Dodge Dart east to Iowa. If you do, you will
be hurled into the dark realms of tow truck
drivers — depraved offspring of Hades and
a Cyclops's named Laciva.**

Davy Boy commenced a bender prior to the next weekend performance, so Student was Officer of the Deck, regards security. The four leviathans were there again, and looked forward to seeing the play once more. Student had not allowed the cast to languish during the week — but kept them in good form, continuing to polish.

Thankfully no members of the John Birch Society were patriotic enough to show up, for his security had the same ¾-sized Louisville Sluggers beneath their red blazers. Fortune blessed them, for both the Friday and Saturday night's performances were abandoned by the FBI. *"Even they need a weekend off now and then,"* allowed Simon.

After the Saturday performance — which brought gate receipts of almost four hundred dollars, and this was the players' receipt night — everyone was far more somber, for they would now all part. The big news was out about Student becoming Ulovna Gulashka's first assistant in Seattle and Sterling's scholarship to the Yale School of Drama, these gave all the cast a feeling of ownership

And Milly talked both up this way and that, not realizing their success was more her than Student, which he would inject into her litany every time. Though they had stopped having sex months before, he would miss Milly equally to Jessica, and he found that a puzzling truth. She was the most striking and impressive woman he had ever encountered after Iowa. Why did he not tell her that?

Yet the beast of necessity shoved him along with an increased pace.

It was now mid-May, and Student knew he needed every week and day until September to get his father off the dime and move south. Student had an unsure feeling about that entire situation. He could not direct his father like he did his cast.

With time running short, each visit with Jessica and the twins became harder, for his departure was set. Jessica began engineering the coming fact of his departure from their life and also easing the girls into moving to New York.

"Children don't do departures very well, especially when there will be no return — the last part being worst. She will see her uncle and cousins again, though. But for you, it's touchier."

"Am I supposed to just vaporize and not exist anymore? We will certainly write, call? Will we not?"

"We shall. But children love too easily and that must have a chance to go away, slowly but sure. I mean, it is a tough call, Student. All of it."

Student supposed she was right, and her procedure commenced with fewer overnights. When they could make love, it was more frenetic and a poignant ambiance inserted itself, which went some ways to work against them.

To Student getting gone was a spectrum wide concept: everyone in San Francisco was leaving his life. The brief resignation letter of his fellowship resulted in silence from Jenkins until late one day at the University when he was packing Jenkins loomed from around the corner of his door.

"You are fortunate, to study and gain experience under

Ulanova Glashka, but what will my wife do for excitement, Student."

When he flopped down in the chair Student saw he was half pickled. When Jenkins looked over and saw the photograph of his office mate's fiancée he reached over and turned it face down.

"So, my boy, when are you leaving?"

"In a week. I'll take my car."

"That *thing* you drive?"

"Yes, but it has a very powerful engine."

"Hmmm. The program will suffer without you. I'll never find a replacement of your caliber. By the way, that scrumptious looking little lady you are now with — where will you file her?"

It might have challenged Student's estimation of how many outrages combined with good will Jenkins was capable of uttering when drinking.

"She is going to New York — she is a writer, and an ambitious one."

He reached into his coat pocket and took out a flask,

"We will toast to your good fortune and abilities."

And they did. When Jenkins was about to leave, he turned and lifted his hand from his waist, and did a farewell wave that described an arc across the doorway. Then Jenkins was out of there.

Student had an urge to chase after him and say, *"I want to thank you for changing my life,"* but did not. He knew it was true and that he should do that. But perhaps the old Student was resuming control — doing sensible things, and saying just enough to stay in a safe zone. It was a flaw he did not want to return. But old ways could not be abandoned so simply.

He caught the bus out to Jessica's feeling that last time, despite catching it early, there was still unresolved tension between them and they weren't out of troubled waters yet. Student, especially at home, lived a life where argument — cross words — were not exchanged. His mother and father taught that antagonism was never necessary for it was a sign of allowing things to go too far. "*Nip them in the bud,*" his father would allow. And, he was right.

So, one tactic was sure: If Jessica wanted to be disagreeable Student wasn't going to make it easy. And his was a good call, for it did not start well.

"Went out to Ocean Beach, walked. It'll be awhile until I see the ocean again."

"Seattle has an ocean, Student, in fact the same one."

Yes, there it was. She was preparing a snack for the girls who were about to arrive off the bus. Jessica thought it OK for him to be here — for it was several days since they'd seen him.

Student disliked this weaning the twins away from him. To the contrary he believed kids their age understood farewells especially when amiable. And why could there not be assurances of future letters and postcards; all children were fond of getting mail, the girls were no exception.

He mustered a stout heart and kept focused on maintaining a peaceful ambiance.

"Since you'll be driving east one month after I will, I would really like you to check in at my parents place and visit me and them. Lots of room for guests. It is only thirty five miles north of the interstate. You know, the Iowa farms — corn will be over your head. It would be a great stop."

She set up plates on the table, shot a sideways look — Student was on the couch — she managed an almost genial tone.

"It appears that their uncle is going to buy us airplane tickets to New York. Anyway, I don't get involved in the middle of rescue efforts when I can only hinder and not help. You'll do all right, Student."

The bait was expertly cast — he was a lunk-headed bass, and the red wiggle-lure with its great trailing hooks was slithering past his maw. Student almost snapped it up whole, but instead, held back.

His mental emergency control center warned, *Dive! Dive! Rig for Silent Running, crash dive to 200 meters!*

Again, a nasty flare of anger escaped from the recesses. One fact sure — he did not want this — did he have to endure it? *I don't have to sit around and take these pot shots, a*nd at once got to his feet. This time, he would yield the battlefield.

"I'll have to excuse myself; it seems."

And was up the stairs and out the door before she could react. He headed for the Pier, then veered away. He supposed he might double back to the appropriate bus stop, but instead threaded his way through several short cuts until he found himself walking along the Embarcadero.

Student conducted a stop and go sulk: Occasionally, he would look down into the bay and fall into a reverie, and each one increased his frustration about the situation rather than mitigate it.

Didn't anyone have sense enough to realize that the *Romance of Student and Debbie* novel was over? They had spent nearly 12 years traveling along its pages, planning houses with open floor designs, central heating, two-entry-way kitchens with white, gleaming do-dads and ovens wafting apple pie with Debbie big with child.

This catalogue confection was obliterated, gone, kaput.

Student wasn't going to rescue anybody; in fact he had

been lucky to rescue himself. The woman Debbie now was, was absolutely a different sort — she had been knocked off the normalcy wagon headfirst into the ditch. And why? Because she was unable to manage without Student being close by for twelve calendar months.

"Most couples don't endure a year apart, Stu."

It took him endless hours that evening and a few to follow to convince her she could easily manipulate her way upon a college campus without his counsel.

So, Student was wrong and she paid for it?

He didn't know what sort of woman might be now occupying Debbie's body. One fact sure, she was smart enough to get the hell out of Kossuth County, and in fact Iowa in general. But that was her problem.

Student was going by different music now, and as chance would have it — and it was chance — he liked this music better than any other.

Jessica?

They were good to each other; he was growing despondent that their last moments were developing into a bitter time. A nagging idea had been lurking: What might be her response if he asked, *"You can write anywhere. Come with me to Seattle. I want to be with you. The girls need a father."*

Going even roughly by what she had declared, her answer would be a 'no,' and an even greater strain would be cast upon his departure. And if she went against her instincts and said 'yes,' then he would be uprooting her three thousand miles from her avowed ambitions. This sacrifice on her part might soon sour.

So, what was he doing? Getting on with it — what other option did he have? And farewells? For Student's money, adults had a much harder time with them as children. And he wanted none of them to sully relationships that were so positive and amiable.

At the very least, he wanted to remember Jessica as the good, lively soul who saved him from the poorest night on personal record, or close to it. How one morning he awakened to find two very strange looking little girls looking him over.

He walked himself thirsty and hungry — having bailed out of Jessica's before eating anything. He saw the Ferry Building clock tower approaching, and knew that *Mr. Scoop* would be close by with his wagon — an ice cream and confection vendor.

Mr. Scoop bought his ice cream from a plant who actually made custom batches daily. Student sighted Mr. Scoop's red and white truck dead ahead: He crossed the street, and set course for its striped awning.

Nearby Jessica sat with the twins.

He imagined it had not been difficult second guessing him.

Since they had introduced him to Mr. Scoop, they were co-addicts. He found himself very glad they had.

He was always buoyed to see them. All of them.

The twins came over to him while he purchased a bold double-decker, and escorted him to the two tables with chairs — Mr. Scoop's portable café. They talked — each twin rapidly over the other — telling him how they knew he would be at Mr. Scoop, and weren't they clever girls indeed?

He absolutely admitted they were sly boots.

By this time he faced off with Jessica who lapped up ice cream between glances at him — a conversation commenced in Ethiopian between the three — a helluva convenient code. Jessica translated; she usually did out of politeness and an interest of international relations, "They know we fought and want me to apologize because they know you would not say bad things. So,

I apologize," she looked to both of them, who acknowledged her obedience with a shared nod. ". . . that was a lousy thing I said, but on the other hand, you might try saying something instead of just walking out, Student."

"If glib enough, I would have said I prefer rescuing you than Deborah, but that you don't need it and I'm too late for her."

"You might have, but glib men are usually dirt piles. You've allowed me to see a man can be a good person, Student Patterson."

The twins looked to both, wondering what it all was about, save that it was serious. At the edge of the precipice their mother and Student had managed a solid peace.

Jessica broke the silence, said a few things in Ethiopian, and the girls —having finished their cones — headed back to the car. When out of earshot, Jessica drew a breath, dabbed a bit of chocolate ice cream off with a napkin and motioned towards the car,

"Why don't you go back with me — probably won't have much of a dinner, having spoiled our appetite here. Watch a movie on television, eat some popcorn, and after the girls are asleep — we can go upstairs and launch each other into orbit."

This temporarily slipped the noose of the approaching farewell and Student went for her plan in its entirety. Her suggestion was superior to staring at the fissures in the ceiling at the *A plus B Hotel*, room thirteen, Butchers' Town.

17.

Student began the morning moving out of the hotel to the Dodge Dart. Davy Boy kept vigil between trips up to the third floor — security being a bothersome situation with an unlocked car in Butchertown.

When done, Davy Boy walked around it, appraising the Dart with his most sober eye. He came to a decision,

"Chances of you making Iowa with this pile of garbage are slim, Student. I know guys who can boost you a helluva lot better set of wheels with complete papers, no problem."

Cruising eastward in a Cadillac, GTO or even a Corvette with bogus documents and a filed-off engine block number was not appealing.

"Davy Boy, I've had the Dart tested, and it's six cylinders are powerful — tight and ready to roll."

"Well, maybe the cylinders are, Student, but the rest is falling apart."

Davy Boy's spirits were down, and after finding a parking place within line-of-sight of Big Lena's Student stopped him just before entering,

"Davy Boy, you ran great security for us — added to our great success. You're good at what you do."

The tormented fellow stopped cold, unused to such words.

"Jesus, thank you Student. We're going to miss you at the guild."

Entering Big Lena's, he and Davy Boy joined Simon for a farewell breakfast. He had much respect for Simon, for he was a good man who had lived his life as he believed. Student benefited from Simon's advice always.

Lena gave Student a hug, and slid in next to Simon, who pushed a leather valise across to him; all three gestured for him to open it.

It was an old script in Russian of *The Lower Depths*, and across the first page was Maxim Gorky's autograph, dated 1928, Moscow.

"Oh, my God."

Student was stupefied. It was like finding a hand-written note from Karl Marx in the mail.

Simon signed to an imaginary fifth party.

"It was Milly's idea — you can thank her later. But, it is not all bad having socialist connections, Student. It's genuine, and information about its provenance — that is the word for it — is inside with it."

"Excuse — a moment."

He made the restroom before tearing up unabashedly. Patterson men simply did not weep in public. Looking at his image in the mirror he steeled himself at once. This was helped by reading "*Nixon eats shit*" written across it.

He wiped away the moisture, and returned, and after profuse thanks, said, "You all are the greatest, most motivated socialists I've ever met, and I'll never forget you."

He made his goodbyes with them. Big Lena gave him a bag of donuts for later, and all watched him climb into the Dart, and cruise away from San Francisco's Butchertown for possibly the last time.

He had definitely put in his time there.

Milly had wanted to do a fully formal British style tea service in her apartment but Student insisted on an all-out sit down dinner.

She choose the *Shanghai Parrot* in Chinatown, not precisely your premier dining trough, but your average San Francisco Chinatown restaurant, complete with red-dragon door pieces and rude waiters.

Milly managed another black dress, with no frills apparent anywhere. Student enjoyed the complete story about where they had found the autographed script, then worked into her plans for the Haywood Playhouse. A sad tone came over her, perhaps one more of longing.

"I want Ruth to be with me for a year, at least. It is the time in her life when it is good to have a mother around."

They talked some about passports and such hurdles. She trailed off the topic with a resigned sigh. They both watched the sexy cocktail waitress on one of her many commutes from the second floor lounge to the tables below, carrying drinks. It was a steep staircase. Student followed her gaze and nodded,

"Yes. The split dress is nice — the guys can look right up it when she walks down, as you can see."

"In a socialist society, Student, such things would not be; we are screaming in the wilderness against such unfairness but one cannot give up."

"Milly, allow this Democrat to segue away from matters socialist, but time is short. I wanted to tell you — you might resist this notion, but you are a very attractive woman."

"Student, don't be silly, boys used to throw dog biscuits at me!"

"I find you attractive, as you know — you should know."

"I'm old now. And Student, you're not the ordinary sort of man."

"You *aren't* old now. And I am an ordinary man. Certainly Ruth's father saw you as attractive. "

"Avi? He is an intensely intelligent and very charming man," she took the napkin that was on her lap and folded it up tightly, ". . . I was with Daddy in Israel when he was teaching there, where he still lives. Avi was taking course work from him. I was Saul Rothstein's daughter. So —" she allowed a resigned sigh — "it was more like having an affair with the professor's homely daughter. And Ruth just happened. I was nearly 30 and it was my first non-socialist, well — *attachment*. So, Student, my being attractive had nothing to do with things."

He was about to continue his stance when the waiter occupied this inappropriate moment to slap the bill with two fortune cookies on the table and hustle back to his pod of fellow waiters at the rear.

Student nabbed the bill, took one of the fortune cookies and read it,

"YOU WILL SOON COME INTO A GREAT DEAL OF MONEY."

He abandoned the shell of the cookie uneaten, saw that Milly had read hers.

"What did it say, Miss Rothstein?"

She held up a finger and warned, "Oh, you can't say, or you'll negate its magic. So don't tell me yours either." She offered a rare smug smile. "I will say mine is quite good."

It rained steadily on their way to the bus stop. He had not taken the Dodge Dart for it was loaded to the gunwales and parking in Chinatown was absurd both from the standpoint of availability and security. They huddled together under her umbrella and once on the bus, Student decided to become forthcoming and unburden himself, at least somewhat.

"I will meet Jessica and the kids tomorrow morning at the Sheraton Palace. I have become close to her two girls, twins. She's going to New York, but by air. I won't be seeing any of them again. Along with not seeing you again, and them — I'm so confused about all these twists and turns — now Seattle and the promises there."

Her expressive olive-dark eyes rested on him, and certainly she guessed what he had omitted — the pain — the worst sort, cloudy and drifting.

"Of course you are confused. I think intelligent good people who push their limits are invariably confused. I am about what I have done and will do." She looked at Student, their bodies leaning back as the bus gamely climbed the hill, cresting the top with a diesel wheeze, ". . . you are theater people now, Student. I can see it in you. We'll spend our whole life staging things that aren't true to make them appear real. What can be more confusing than that?'

They rode on in the rain and Student at once countermanded her when she suggested they make their farewells on the bus.

"Baloney! I will escort my date to her doorstep."

They stepped off and watched the unfortunate bus hobble off — an ancient pachyderm at end of life.

They confronted her door. Student knew at once why it might have been better to make farewells on the bus. They stood there, examining the placid face of her door as if an intriguing encyclopedia passage were writ in large letters upon it.

"Student, we have done this well, have we not? This farewell? If we are confused now —" she looked back, as if a reporter might be taking note, then directly to him — "Women can be as deceptive as men. I *never* work out bourgeois tensions with any man, but I do upon occasion see one I desire." She put the umbrella down, took his head between her hands. "One thing absolute, Student Patterson, if you have trouble up north, or just need a reassuring soul, say the word, and I will be there."

He tried to say the same back, but she kissed him firmly,

opened her door and was gone. This moment taught him hurt Student hadn't known; he could not be sure if the lesson were good or bad.

18.

It was a well-intended idea to have a farewell brunch at the Sheraton Palace Hotel, but he saw it was not right. The twins were ill at ease and Jessica too, for this wasn't their sort of place, nor was it Student's. While the twins argued about the animals on the wallpaper, sotto voce, Jessica managed, "They are becoming more aware that their skin color is different than others."

Indeed, no black people were customers in the capacious dining room, and only a few as workers. Student was asked to adjudicate zoological issues for the girls: Were they horses or goats on the wallpaper?

"Horses, girls."

They always moved him to good humor and he needed it now. Like Jessica he was beat — he pled sleeplessness and fatigue due to all the preparations for today's departure.

As he had waited for Jessica and girls this morning in the foyer, he wondered again if he loved her or for that matter Milly. Then, with a frightening snippet of trepidation, if he loved *anyone* beyond his parents?

He felt flawed. At thirty, Student should have begun spending his allotted supply of love — which he often theorized was a non-renewable expenditure.

At that point in his reverie, he watched Jessica and her twins walk in — dressed '*to the nines,*' as they say, and Student wondered if parting from them was almost too much to bear. After all, ironically — this is what Debbie pled when he opted for a year at sea.

He felt a precarious handhold slipping away.

They now ate — the twins shepherded through the Sheraton

Palace protocols by Jessica.

"Girls, not from the jam container to the mouth — from the container to the toast, *then* eat the toast."

Student and Jessica looked at each other, and he suddenly had an off-putting premonition — for himself, but not her.

"I think, after this morning, I will be next seeing you in Seattle while I stand in a line at a book signing. I'm sure of it."

Jessica brightened, for she was ambitious and doing increasingly well as a writer. Student was sure she would do well — always.

They walked to his Dart — the rear seat stuffed to the rim with belongings.

"Oh, Student, you will drive all that way in this? How exciting, isn't that true, mother?"

They looked into each window on the curb side, while Jessica and he maintained an eye-lock on each other. Her eyes —her entire continence — remained steady. Student found words coming out in wounded pieces.

"This is heavy weather, Jessica. You always brought something good to me, and I'm grateful. You are a fine human being and I'm a better person for being with you, even for a while."

She said something in Ethiopian to the girls and they walked away obediently and looked into a shop window,

"If one doesn't weep, and I don't, that doesn't mean being unfeeling, or worse, unknowing. Remember Student, I think you are a good person and man. Until I met you, I thought men all came equipped with a missing part. I was so damned glad you didn't ask me to give it all up and go to Seattle with you. That would have been just awful."

And she went forward, kissed him then called the girls forward.

"Now, say goodbye to Student. He will be writing you, won't you?"

"Of course. First, two pop up books from Iowa; special Iowa pop up books."

And he kissed each of them, and lamented from the roots of his hair down to his feet that he wasn't their father.

And then, he got in the Dart, and drove off.

Confused with a swarm of conflicting thoughts he missed the on-ramp to the Bay Bridge, and doubled back to pick it up. It was a cool San Francisco late spring morning. Maneuvering onto the bridge, the sparse traffic reminded him it was a Sunday in early June. Student had been in San Francisco one year.

Part Two

Deus Ex Iowa

1.

Student pulled into his parents' farm six days eighteen hours after leaving San Francisco. Casualties had been moderate: two breakdowns and three flat tires, but contrary to predictions the 1961 Dart (modified) made it to Iowa, albeit with numerous *oomphs* and *ahhhhs*.

In Reno, Nevada, he was passed by his own drive shaft. Almost through Utah, the axle assembly came out from the differential while he was just pulling off the road to fix a flat tire on the front.

At each emergency stop impressed locals would watch Student as he remounted his strange freshly repaired conveyance to hobble off down the interstate, an intrepid animal migrating home.

"My God, Student! Why didn't you tell us. We would have sent money."

It was his mother and not his father who backed away from the Dart after the initial whoop-te-do of greeting — as if it might suddenly flip over backwards, landing on its carapace, dead.

Father, Mother, and Son reunited in a grand manner. Without a doubt, Student's return to a place where human events happened in a placid and civilized manner was a grateful return to the Americana of old *Saturday Evening Posts*. No dynamite-loving eccentrics or ax/bare fist combatants.

Aunt Lila was called at once, and within 10 minutes she appeared — joining the Patterson family hugging extravaganza. Initially, she hadn't realized that the object of diverse metal parts before her was his means of transport during the last 2,000 miles. Lila was more positive.

"Student, you have a car with a steering like our postman."

Things calmed after dinner, and he was able to retreat with his father to the hatchery. His news-of-the-times nibbled around the corners of the Debbie situation, and then moved focus to her parents: Mother and Father were separated due to the conflict over the grand-daughter. He was great material for the *Grand Leatherhead of the Year* award, in his Dad's opinion.

"Harold, well you know, is Presbyterian elder through and through."

His father allowed criticism to stop there. They sipped brandy while his father glued together tiny pieces dissected from the internal workings of one of the ancient incubators. The entire batch of Patterson egg incubators, Student supposed, were purchased by the original owner not long after the advent of electricity in agriculture.

His father kept them going *('They're as good as new, if you know their inner-workings')*; the tiny paint brush dabbed and inserted dashes of glue in just the right place; his father wore jeweler's magnifiers attached to his glasses.

With these two pair of specs, he looked not only like an owl, but one with poor vision.

He stopped, described several ovals in the air with the brush as he searched for words concise enough to voice his thoughts. While doing so, he dipped it daintily in the glue — working on these parts was like breathing. He was able to converse about many other thoughts and still work with precision.

"So, do you plan to meet Debbie? There is wonder about that herein."

The brush worked its intricacies, then he raised it again and described a few more ovals in the air with it, looking at him through numerous lenses. It was a wonder to watch father and son communicate, for mostly it was not done with words — or very few.

". . . you know. You *are* going to see her, I assume?"

"Yes."

"Good, that's good."

Carefully he put the part down, then laid the brush in a tray, bristles up. Taking the glass of brandy between thumb and two fingers he sipped — thought — sipped. Put it down.

"So?"

"So what?"

"Your mother has suggested a dinner. You know, us, her, Lila, and Debbie, and the infant, of course."

"No. Awkward."

"Awkward."

He muttered that, picked up his work and resumed.

"You know one of the cast members I sacked tried to beat me to death and I had to defend myself with a fire ax."

Down went the brush and part again, and he put a hand to both knees.

"The hell?! A fire ax?"

"Yes. Lucky I remembered it was there."

"You think directing plays will be that —" he picked up the glass, sipped and offered — "brawny a task in Seattle? You know, lumberjacks and such?"

"No, at least it has not been mentioned. Wouldn't expect rough stuff in a former neighborhood church — the Btuchers Town Writer's Guild was something else again."

"That is behind you. But there were good people there too?"

"Yes. Quite a few." He stood and picked up a stack of magazines realizing he had nothing to read for that evening, so why not chickens, "I thought I would go over to where Debbie is staying and have coffee and just — you know, make a low-pressure, casual visit out of it."

His father drew a breath — a man hard put to carry on nasty duty as messenger figure.

"In that case, I'm sorry to relay Debbie prefers Lila and us being actually present."

"What!?"

He tossed the magazines down and gestured towards outside, tried to say something, but instead bit a lip and shook his head. His father carefully took up the part and brush.

Student calmed by sorting through his priorities. The top objective was getting his father and mother packed up and ready for the movers by September first — in two months 20 days.

There were enough problems right here.

For starters, his mother's letter was accurate; his father seemed to be operating on a vastly different time scale, possibly on Mars or Jupiter time. Student did not need to compound things by dealing with the foibles of a misfired flower child.

He was going to enjoy these days at home, his mother and father in surroundings so predictable.

"I'm beat, Dad. The brandy did it. God help me, driving that Dart was like riding inside an oil filter."

"Oh, I would think."

Student hugged him — and the elder tried to return it, but was caught short in mid-task, but he did his best, putting both arms over Student's shoulders, with an incubator part in each hand. Student felt like a pigeon, freshly arrived at his home roost.

"I'm extraordinarily happy to be home and see you both."

Yet he hadn't been exaggerating, for with topnotch food and brandy inside, fatigue overwhelmed.

Lila was gone and his mother was doing dishes — he came up behind her, lifted her, and after giving her a hug, headed for his second story bedroom,

"Did you have other girlfriends in San Francisco, Dear?

Can a mother ask that? Is that OK nowadays?"

Student should have known he would not make it upstairs that easily — his mother was a person of language and information, and he was her son.

"Yes. Named Jessica."

"Serious?"

"Well, rather. Yes, She had two children. Twins. Beautiful little girls."

There were questions and answers about the twins, and she hung up the dish towel and leaned against the counter.

"She is an ambitious writer — wants to be a novelist, and will be flying to New York — moving there within a few weeks."

"Did you love her?"

He decided answering straight-on.

"Mom, during the last two years, I've been doing good to love you guys. Beyond that, the topic of love is a real puzzle."

"Oh, Student. Don't say that, dear. You have been in the city too much, is all."

She believed a harsh urban world excised goodness from people. She had attended business college in Chicago for six months. That did it.

In his bedroom, he got ready for bed, and since the room was scrunched in the corner of the second floor, it reminded him of Milly's room beneath the stairs. He would miss her — did miss her. And badly.

Student became disgruntled. To think Debbie was so out of kilter she could not trust him not to say something wicked. They had known each other for fifteen years and he had never said a harsh word to her. She knew he disdained her pig-headed father who too often offered derogatory remarks about his father.

Well screw him.

He crawled into bed, and enjoyed the old sounds of the

house- — audible as his mother worked at something or other below. As so many times in his life — thousands — she began to hum a tune. And she had a sweet, in-tune voice, and he went to sleep listening, and why not? Was not this soft voice the first sound he had ever heard?

During the ensuing days he discovered to no surprise whatsoever that his father was involved with serious heel dragging regards the move to Florida. His parents clearly had contrasting migratory urgings.

Student's parents' respective estimates of the job ahead varied — from wildly to almost irrational, mostly on his father's part.

His father was convinced that he and the Parks brothers, with Student helping and supervising, could wrap up the entire farm in 30 days. His mother and Aunt Lila sat at the table when she visited again—her mother speaking of reality to both Lila and Student.

"He and Student couldn't pack our place up in two months, and with the Parks brothers they would just help Arthur waste time. It is an entirely self-defeating plan."

The topic of Debbie was avoided with his mother present. Certainly his father relayed Student's thoughts that a group dinner was not a good idea.

Finally when alone with Aunt Lila, the *Debbie topic* came up — as it would.

"Student, Debbie won't meet you alone. Now don't get angry! I don't know *why*. I told her you would never say anything ill about her or *to* her. But that is what she says. She went through a real hell with those parents of hers, and it still goes on. Her labor was an awful thing; I wasn't comfortable that only a midwife was present — not at all. But her father washed his hands of her financially, the rat."

Lila and he took in a movie, and afterwards threaded their way through Lila's smitten, silver-haired swains who vied for a word with her. Also, a few locals welcomed back Student, about whose 'success' they heard. No one mentioned Debbie who had brought good Christian people disgrace by unspeakable behavior.

The following days he spent re-acclimatizing from the coast — the late June days were climbing into the high 90's already — he began early maneuvers to find a workable plan to reconcile his parents' varying views on Florida.

It was not fast work but Student enjoyed it. In truth, he could not come to tell his mother he never thought his father was a prime Florida retiree. The debate remained within the family — no outsider would know the Patterson's were not on the same chapter regards fun in the sun.

The "Bread Lady" was a new addition to the community of farms.

She stopped by their place on a Wednesday. She had a box built on the back of a pickup decorated with various cut-out wooden animals where rested bread and other bakery items — all wonderful. It was a strange but successful idea — selling homemade bread to farm women who no longer took time for home baking.

Looking her goods over while she delivered two loaves to his Mom, Student also looked her over, and she him. She was a tall woman, an age difficult to assess. She wore a long batik dress and had brown hair down to her waist — right down the middle of it was a light streak of gray.

She wore wire-rimmed glasses behind which were green eyes. Student immediately thought of the Homeric translation —

'*dancing-eyed women*', and she was all of that.

She was a glaring example of counterculture spill-over.

"You're Beverly's son? Student? You have been in San Francisco?"

And he acknowledged all of these things, and the bread lady did a fetching and miniature few dance steps while singing a snippet of "*If you go to San Francisco,*" an anthem.

"Stop by my place for coffee and rolls; I lived in San Francisco for two years, well — close to it. I'd love to get updated — that was several years ago. Weekends are best, any time."

After she drove off, his mother sniffed the bread, acknowledged it as the best she'd tasted. She added the bread lady rented the old five-acre Johnson place and arrived equipped with a couple of children and a number of pets. She was originally a Pellison.

"The oldest girl."

That — for his mother — said it all. The Pellison family were notorious throughout the county for troubles diverse.

The entire topic of women decided things for Student about a plan concerning Debbie. He knew that an approach with the right mixture of the casual and diplomatic would work best. With luck, it would last less than an hour. Student must be, not seem, a now platonic friend who held no ill will and wished her good fortune.

He waited for the next day.

In late morning, he confessed a nostalgia for fishing in the creek. His mother was always up on matters of local health.

"But the fisheries people say we can't eat the fish. They're full of chemicals from the fields."

"I'll return them fat and happy."

He got his old straw hat, picked up a pole, line, and tackle from the storage trailer, and digging enough worms to make it look serious, took off down-road, pole over his shoulder.

He hiked to the creek, turned up the county road where he was still visible from his house — the corn was only shoulder high so he was still visible. He took his old path down to the creek.

Now he was out of view.

The county's backroads, sideroads, trails and paths were embossed upon his mind since he was ten, and he didn't have to calculate distances. Instinct informed he would cut off three miles to where Debbie stayed. At the old field bridge — long collapsed —he hid his fishing pole and gear, and struck out overland.

Corn was planted in seamless miles in every direction, interrupted only by county or private roads. The day was not as hot as the previous, and there was a slight breeze tossing the corn gently — causing a rustle. In a small irrigation ditch leading from the creek, black birds sang, took flight and looped up and back down again. Swallows searched out bugs over the fields and meadowlarks occupied any high spot, their refrain reminding all within range of their presence.

Student reminded himself this was a bountiful country, each summer almost erasing out the memory of winters preceding and the anxiety of those to follow. Iowans excelled at forgetting all winters yet paradoxically recalling and discussing in depth any one of them.

He emerged from the fields and ditches right on the button: He was a quarter mile from Debbie's place. He stood at the fork of her uncle's road — the larger of the two snaking between the corn fields to the left. That direction led to her uncle's forbidding shiplap house.

In that manor house, frugality was the absolute highest praise to God.

He was Debbie's mother's brother; this frail tendril of

kinship explained why he shook loose with shelter for his disgraced niece. Also, it was a very private place — away from human eyes. Here, his uncle knew, a woman guilty of fornication could befoul her hair with dirt, tear out hanks of it — and generally cringe before God's disapproving eyes.

Student took the right fork, and came into view of a small house. Only then did he experience a twinge of apprehension — it had been almost two years to the day since he said farewell to Debbie at the train station.

Though she held it together until the final hour, she had been absolutely miserable.

He slowed — looking over the place. She was there, the evidence being old beater car was parked under the oak tree, one of its doors still open — Debbie's trademark, a boon to battery manufacturers. Under the spreading greenery of a venerable oak, two stout ropes led down to a baby swing fully equipped with baby. Student halted, as if he had spotted a bear cub. Debbie was within feet of that baby.

Indeed, she exited the door carrying a bucket one-handed, and labored down the stairs with it. To Student she looked — despite the load and disarray from her task, striking — which she always managed without trying.

When she espied him, she put down the bucket of a sudden and stared, unmoving. Student resumed some forward movement and tried out a smile — lifted an arm in a modest greeting. There was no attempt at a return gesture; he took a neutral approach and leaned against the edge of a picnic table.

"Hello, Debbie."

"Stu. Oh, I don't know about this."

"Why not? I heard you feared meeting me alone. Why on earth would you? I have never said or done anything to harm or discomfort you, and I won't start now, for God's sakes."

He heard a quiet little tune, and when he looked for its source, saw that the swing holding the infant had one of those devices that swayed it gently and played a lullaby.

"That is Juanita. You might as well see her."

She went over and he followed. Sure enough, the baby Juanita was very dark. She reminded Student of a Smithsonian photograph of an Indian infant on its mother's back, asleep — without concern for thorny problems that plagued all mankind.

"She is quite beautiful."

They withdrew, Debbie back to where she set down the bucket. She wrapped her arms around her torso and shook her head. She had dark brown eyes, and they fixed on him.

"Why didn't you do what I preferred? I don't know about this."

"What on earth are you talking about? Why might I say something to bring harm or pain?"

"Not you. *Me.* I'm afraid of me, wouldn't you think I might be, for God's sakes?"

She looked momentarily to the sky, then bore back down directly on him with eyes that were beginning to narrow. Student began to have an inkling his plan might have been a poor call. When she looked skyward she was Debbie, but when her gaze returned directly on him she had transformed to a blend of Medea and Maggie-the-Cat.

"By the way, Stu, how was your year at sea?"

So, there it was. He felt a touch of the same dread when O'Malley slammed him up against the wall at the BTWG hall.

"Debbie, perhaps we should not discuss my year at sea."

"No. I want to. You're here. *How was your year at sea, Stu?*"

She vocally stepped into those lines with baleful tones — it vaporized his thought that issues would be calmly sorted through. She was a hawk leaning forward — ready to pounce. It was not a matter if she would attack, rather a matter where she might sink her talons.

"You remember how I pled with you not to go to sea. How we had never been apart; how I absolutely begged you not to sign up?"

"Debbie, slow down, I —"

"No! I *won't* slow down. We were betrothed; a man looks after the needs of the woman who is going to have his children. And what had you done!? You told me you had *already* signed up, and would be leaving in two weeks. *You had already signed up*. So, persuading me was just theater for the pliant female — you made the command decision to sail off and play *The Ancient Mariner*. Yes! And leave the dumb corn-raised cutie on the shelf for 12 months."

"You mean, I am your villain, responsible for all your woes in two years!?"

He extended his hand, as if trying to ward off the wicked pelting of her words.

"Remember your sage departing advice, Student? That I should watch out for guys lying — you didn't say that included you."

She picked up the bucket again as if to continue her task. But at once he saw she was coming straight at him. Yes! He had plenty of time to duck, but mentally flatfooted from the outrageousness of her rhetoric he froze, she then had time to dump the bucket load of unidentified liquid over his head.

She then hurled the bucket against the side of the house. Student shot to his feet and sputtered,

"What is wrong with you?! Have you gone insane?!"

"I trusted you, Stu. I really trusted you. I was green and afraid to be alone and I said I was afraid of that. I was afraid what might happen at the University by myself, with nobody I knew around. I trusted you, you bastard! Now get out. *Get out!"*

He fled with her words at his back, not believing the scene that had unfurled. He found his way back to the creek and followed it along, wading under the bridge where he hid his fishing pole.

Indignation was now taking over.

He was beginning to dry out, and it was apparent she used a bucket of used laundry water — as if she planned this humiliation. The liquid was rank.

He stripped while muttering uncharacteristic obscenities.

Ignoring the already violated fish population, he bathed himself in the creek, then tried to do what he could with his cutoffs, tee, and canvas runners, but his nakedness soon attracted swarms of greedy, biting gnats.

He wrung out his clothes replaced them and proceeded home. He must accept this afternoon's vengeful "Debbie" was the same Debbie of two years before. And this Debbie affixed her fall from grace and subsequent miseries on Student.

Outrageous.

Of course he had warned her against men! For God's sakes, she did have corn growing out of her ears and never attended university with a large campus.

And the navies of the world do not give their junior officers a week or three to consult their fiancée about a possible new assignment.

He became angrier as he shucked his clothes at the washer, showered, put on fresh clothes and left the house and retired to his fort.

Student needed his fort like no other time.

Everyone should have one, and his was semi-perfect and his parents understood it. Years before, they had traded a load of stewing hens for an old 40 foot long travel trailer, and his father used it for 'storage overflow.' Hence as a teenager Student converted one end of it to his fort. He had burrowed through twenty-five feet of the trailer to the end where there was a double bed and table, a perfect beginning.

So, Student's fort was a narrow tunnel through a vast storehouse of shelves with tagged items, for his father was a believer in tagging everything and inventorying it. *"I will not have unidentified things about."* he would lecture him, *". . . I am not a packrat."*

But he was a packrat. And Student benefited from this fort — for it also had a "secret" entrance, a small door on the abode end, once boarded over.

He went there in earnest: His father and mother observed a sacred trust — the warehouse end remained the warehouse, and the fort remained Student's fort.

This was his castle and keep when the Saracens were outside waiting to nab him. And now they included Debbie.

He crawled into his bed and above it was another bunk he had converted into a small library still holding his childhood favorites; he took a copy of Robert Louis Stevenson's *Jekyll and Mr. Hyde* and decided it was just right.

Student would stay in his fort until reasonably sure hell was freezing around the edges. With his anger a vast chunk of libido peeled free: With this came sexual desire — the sort Scythian looters or Visigoths experienced upon breach of town walls.

Well then, Student took fresh resolve: After re-re-reading *Dr. Jekyll and Mr. Hyde*, he would look up the bread lady and talk about San Francisco and all topics therein.

On the morning of the second day, his mother approached close to the pump house, and then — according to long established protocol — communicated by shouting.

"Student. Are you in there? I saw the light on and last night you raided the refrigerator."

"Yes."

"Do you want to come in and have a hot breakfast?"

"Not really."

"Student, we want you to come in and have breakfast."

"No. Maybe lunch. I'm doing research for the one-act competitions in Des Moines; remember, I told Miss Glashka I would take it in. My new job will have much to do with seeking new material."

Now her voice rose, and he felt the unmistakable hook of maternal authority.

"Student! This is ridiculous. You don't even know what the plays are. Now, I want you to come out and tell us what happened. After all, we are involved too."

He put on clothes and went in. Theirs was not a family that did not mix business, gossip with eating. So, he told them, but now he expanded a bit on what had turned out inexplicably to be a massive issue — he and Debbie's discussion of him going to sea. It seemed that Debbie had not told any of his family about *that night* until yesterday, when she showed up at Lila's '*in emotional pieces.*'

"We met at our favorite restaurant close to the base."

Student's father nodded respectively as the narrative developed though his mother sniffed around at the edges of his story,

"And you really signed up first and told her second?"

"I think I suggested this option several times that week when we talked by phone. I was in the *navy*. I got three months knocked off my last year. They were desperate for officers with deck ratings. I told her that."

"*Before* you signed up?"

"As I said, Mother, I think I intimated it by phone before the dinner."

Finally, his father reached a saturation level for the investigation. He was his son's loyal wing man, and knew his son was in the process of allowing womenfolk to slip behind him where they would shoot his tail section to pieces.

"Beverly, that will do. We shouldn't be grilling our own son about what he did or did not do, especially something that was his right and duty to do. Fact is, Debbie went way overboard. She took a terrible beating here, and is just not thinking clearly. She saw in Student someone to blame, rather than that collection of Puritans and semi-anchorites she has for relatives."

Relieved to be bailed out he collected snacks to eat later, a few more books, that morning's paper — and returned to the sanctity of his fort. He knew he was supposed to be helping with their problems, but for a time, he had his own network of tangles to sort through.

The day rang in hotter than ever, and he closed all the windows of his fort, and turned on his pride and glory — a window model squirrel cage, a water cooler, that blew relief inward along with an occasional gust of scrambled gnats and droplets of water from a leaky line.

And more than anything, the electric motor made a steady rising and settling hum. Since the trailer was beneath two massive black maples that together formed a canopy spanning over a 100 feet, his fort next to the old pump house was cool and quiet. He could listen to the water cooler's motor as it rose, and settled- — regularly. And in the heat of the day, he would nod off, forgetting the reptilian nastiness of the world.

Like any good Spanish Duke, he slept through the heat of the day. In the evening he read snippets in the "Iowa Chit-Chat" column, including the birth of calves with odd birth marks, and the lush growth of corn from a field not planted.

Student would read anything rather than ruminate on his utter humiliation — how he had just stood there like a lump of dough allowing her to dump the unspeakably foul water over him.

He looked out at Neon, the Patterson dog, who slept under the water-outflow of the cooler — his own long-ago tactic to avoid the heat.

It was all very peaceful as the sun began sinking, and there would follow a time of day when the heat would back off — hours that were a balm to daytime concerns.

He nodded off and was awakened with a knock on the rear entrance, and his father's voice.

"Student, may I enter your lair?"

His father had never been in his fort — in fact, he and his Dad never occupied the entire structure simultaneously out of mutual respect: When his Dad stashed and labeled his stuff here, it was a great solitary pleasure and it was the same with Student's fort, and they both understood.

This was not just a first — but a major first.

"Of course. Enter with honor."

He did, closed the door very softly behind, as he might in church.

"Debbie is here and wants to see you. She's very contrite."

Student withdrew under his covers. His father sat, looked over the squirrel cage cooler and segued gladly to this device.

"Oh, that is terrific, Student. Made for an area five times this. Really sucks in the bugs too, all plastered against the outside filters."

"Whole thing cost five bucks at *Walters Junk.*"

They both admired it. Student knew he had to muster some response.

"I don't know if I want to see her. I think she's gone mental."

His father — and Student knew he had a miserable assignment — put his hands on each knee and nodded. At one time years ago, he smoked a pipe but gave it up — and back then, when matters went serious, the pipe would always get loaded up and set off like a smudge pot.

Student could read him better than anyone, and vice versa. His Dad craved his pipe now equal to just getting the hell gone.

"So, do you want me to tell them that?"

"Them? Is Aunt Lila here too?"

"No, but she's in on it even though your mother and Debbie says she isn't."

"So, she's come to apologize?"

"I can't say." A smile began — a first a hint of one, then a full version and the sly glint. "She's not carrying a bucket, though."

They both enjoyed that a bit, and Student inhaled and knew he was in a tight corner. There was no gentle escape, but by God he would not budge from his fort.

"OK. But here. She beseeches me in *my* place. And if she doesn't have a Homeric-grade apology ready, she's out of here. I'm not going to argue over the syntax of a discussion we had *two years ago!*"

He uncharacteristically raised his voice a bit, and his father nodded, and was about to exit, but instead turned,

"I'll so convey, but I have to say, that she had an appalling time. Her father made a bad situation absolutely wretched, and has beaten everybody to a pulp with that version of Christianity he carries around in his wallet. Debbie, still naive in many ways, was innocent enough to come home and think he would be accepting,"

Then exited. This was indeed an exceptional evening — another first. Student rarely heard his dad speak derogatorily about a neighbor's — or anyone's — religion.

Student withdrew into the corner confident he poisoned the deal, then the next second hoped he had not. If the woman he experienced the other day was filled with the quantity of venom demonstrated, she might not suck down enough pride and anger to enter his space. It had been years since she'd been here.

The motor on the cooler prevented hearing her approach and instead of the back door, she knocked on the front.

This necessitated him moving. Naked because of the heat, he struggled to put on shorts, stooped and passed through the narrow gerbil-like passage formed by his father's stock of inventory. There was another modest knock at the front door.

When he opened it, a baby carry-all complete with baby was shoved at him,

"Take her Stu. There's gnats everywhere out here. There has been a hatch of them. They're in my hair!"

Not having a humanitarian choice, he took the baby Juanita, while Debbie whirled in full combat, carrying a pack of baby supplies.

"God, I hate gnats. I'm sorry."

And she closed the door behind her, back against it. They confronted. She reached out and relieved him of the baby, holding it in one hand and the pack in the other.

"I know this is abrupt."

"Yes."

He turned and with her following for the return trip — squeezing between all the hoarded material — climbed up into bed, drew a sheet over him, and crept into the corner far as possible. From there he scrutinized this extraordinary visitor in the event she sneaked by the check point armed. She appraised his "office" stool, and sat. She bounced the infant Juanita a bit, though she was quiet. There was a time when Debbie was an honored and frequent guest in his fort.

"I've thought quite a lot about what I did, and I wanted to stop by and tender my deepest regrets for —" she dangled a handout for a moment, fill in the blank style — "it was a dreadful thing to do. Your family, all of them, helped me when no others would; when no others cared, even my own parents. And you are their son, and after all Juanita isn't your doing."

She batted at her hair with a free hand,

"Gnats in my hair. *I hate them*," She shook her hair, and Student marveled at the fullness of it, and also she had taken to not wearing an undergarment. She was as voluptuous as any rural bread lady. He struggled against all that.

"So, you're apologizing for dumping a bucket of slop over me?"

"I do regret it. Yes."

Student did not hear an apology, for regrets were not an apology, and since they were both word people, she knew it.

"Was it Aunt Lila's idea to apologize to me?"

"No! It was *not*. She was not happy about what I did, but understood. This is my idea, wholly, and . . ."

But she didn't finish with the anticipated '. . . *and I wasn't apologizing.*' She just decelerated to a stop. Student stayed cautiously huddled beneath the sheet. She looked around, and nodded — remembering the interior of his fort well. They had sneaked in here often, he in the first year of high school, her just entering middle school — he had first talked her out of her clothes here.

There was extensive exploring through all that, up to and through high school. They had talked all sorts of plans—places they might travel during summers off, and most of all their future together — possibly until they were both 100 years old.

"Maybe we're vampires," he would say, *"and we'll live for centuuries."*

That was forever ago. Those dreams slipped by during this two year renaissance.

She stared at the window cooler, a recent addition, cupping her hand and moving air towards her.

"That's nice."

Student readied a sarcastic remark, struggling to maintain a mojo of nastiness. He was angling how best to nail her equivocating hide to the wall over the non-apology. He was betting she'd either said or suggested that apologizing was her intention.

Now, she'd backed out.

Yet the memory of this woman's anger was too recent. The stench of the slop remained lodged in his sniffer. The ugly scene at her uncle's had been such a new — actually, strange Debbie — Student was hesitant to dicker over words. Better — safer — for the moment to stick to the cooler.

"I got it at a junk yard — in pieces. I fixed it."
"Oh!"

It was an impressed 'oh,' for he wasn't keen on fixing things. Late evening shadows reached into his fort, and they were both cast in them. The lush canopy overhead held in the moisture, creating a hollowness to sounds from outside.

In this sort of ambiance, Student marveled that Debbie looked all the world like a daguerreotype portrait of 'woman and child' from the dawn of art photography in France or Italy.

She reached out, confirmed that the infant was asleep, then

put Juanita and carrier over on the table, first making sure it was stable. She shoved her pack of baby things beneath.

"Your father did tell me you thought I had lost my sanity or something over the top like that."

"It's true."

"Well, I haven't. I thought a few months earlier I might."

Student and she sat then in silence as they had so many times — usually reading, sometimes reading to each other. Other times just lazing about and dreaming. She fiddled with the blanket around Juanita, and he thought back over the previous two years — and especially the previous year. His reflective sweep was done at a speed across electrical circuitry only possible in the human mind.

And of all the images from that chunk of time, the one that froze in a tableaux was of Eddy dead, the television playing a soap opera before his leaden eyes. And at his side Mrs. Smith lecturing, not realizing Eddy had departed the sordid world that was the *A plus B Hotel*. It was such a solitary image that at this particular moment, it frightened Student.

"Debbie, I've seen the strangest things, harsh, and I'm sure you have too."

"In Vietnam?"

"Oh, no. The part of town where the theater was in San Francisco. It was in a seedy area. No flower children or free love there."

She wondered about the irony of that, but did not pursue, then gazed sadly down at the floor.

"I'm so sorry, Stu."

She crossed her legs, and as was a lifelong habit, moved her toe that was free of the floor slowly up and down — always a sign of being both troubled and thoughtful.

Up and down went the tip of her moccasin — and she stared

at it. Then looked up.

"Except for Juanita and getting my special education certificate, the entire year and a half in Wisconsin was *fucked*."

Student put a bit of melodrama into being startled — opening his eyes wider. He allowed a half-smile.

"*Deborah!* Did you use such language at home?"

"No, events went badly enough there without the 'f' word. But an ugly word conveys an ugly experience, Stu. And it was."

With an agile turn-of-mind Student went head-on with the situation *now*: He was not involved in memory-time, but a brief portal when he must make up his mind now and do it fast. He had to stop wading around in events that *were* or those that *should have been*.

He looked squarely at her — drew himself up and like many great warriors entering the battlefield, decided this was a good day to die, rhetorically speaking. It was not a matter of admitting wrong, but of recognizing the timing and appropriateness.

"I want to apologize for telling you I was *thinking* of doing a year at sea, when I had already decided. I just thought I could convince you fully."

She looked at him — then back at the tip of her shoe. Uncrossing he legs, she put both feet flat on the floor, rested a hand on the baby carrier and allowed,

"And I apologize for throwing a bucket of slop-water on you."

With their bitter and mutual diplomacies out of the way, she leaned towards him and continued,

"Student, I still love you, but it is now entirely different, and somehow it has gotten mixed in with a lot of anger about life as it is out there. And this awfulness with my parents did nothing to improve it. Things have come so far since the poetry club."

Now the canary was loose from its cage.

"Debbie, looking back, we said we loved each other a thousand times, but it was like rainwater off a duck's back regards the now."

"And I must think of Juanita, and a man not her father ever caring for her."

Student looked at the tiny creature. She was absolutely crashed out, soaring into the lofty places babies went when asleep, unattainable by an older child and certainly an adult.

"Men? I can only speak for myself. I could come to love her like I do the mother; I almost have now."

These words escaped from safe cover — spring hares emerging recklessly from a warren. Student certainly thought about his apology before saying it, but not this declaration. He felt the earnestness of his words increase in energy in the evening calm. Debbie crossed her legs, and looked down at her foot — resuming its usual motion. She stared at the tip of the shoe, her brow furrowing.

The frogs that thrived in the vicinity of the leaky pump house kicked in, inviting the creatures in the massive maple canopy to join, and they did. It was now more darkness than light as this orchestra's various sections joined in.

She stood, checked on the infant, then boosted herself up to the bed, slid in and leaned against him, and that felt marvelous to him.

He indeed understood that for two full years they absented themselves from each other's lives. Both were not privy or in any way informed about what the other was doing or did, except in the most general way.

Some profound changes were obvious — Juanita being the grandest, Student's swerve from teaching to theater a poor second.

At the launch of those two years fate did a slipshod job,

sending them into murky polluted seas rife with boring worms.

"Debbie, if we're going to bring up delicate events, you know, over the last two years, we should . . ."

"Delicate events? Sexual? Why bring them up at all? I feel the difference in you, right now. And you me, surely. We both wanted each other the first few minutes I was here."

"Right enough, surely."

Student thought of the poignant passage in *The Odyssey*, when the Gods took the night when Penelope and Odysseus finally were abed after 20 years, and stretched the hours out into days.

When he shared that literary allusion, she just sighed — there was something of the old chuckle.

"You're hopeless. Don't you see, Penelope was Penelope, and I am no Penelope, and neither can I visualize you tying yourself to the mast. I have gotten awfully practical, Stu." She leaned closer, moved over a tad. ". . . I'm so tired. Tired. I have been through awful things and I'm tired."

She looked over at Juanita and nodded. "She really pigged out just before, in the kitchen. I was talking with your Mom. Your father —" she craned her head back, looked at Student "—how did he do? He is such a special, gentle spirit."

"Actually, he did rather well."

"Oh, I'm thankful."

And he looked down at her and watched her fall asleep. He imagined her moving along through various levels of slumber, until perhaps she reached back to when they *were* in the poetry club together: They *were* into exploring each other's bodies; they *were* into a sort of love that was akin to the greenest of leaves in the earliest time of spring.

Student looked up, and listened for "His Majesty." When they were kids, they would sit and listen to the frogs and katydids — sure they could hear the loudest, most persistent of them all. They called him "His Majesty."

This was their special creature and they would spin stories around him, some historical, some just made up. Listening intently, Student heard him, then wondered how he might tell the difference between His Majesty and Her Majesty. He glanced at Debbie, but she was now quite asleep, and he was glad for her.

They could discuss that later, and it would be an interesting discussion indeed, and all such following. For so many things given to them were a wonder, and these previous two years certainly showed that.

And how could this wonder have been if it weren't for the Gods or God allowing a victory to be granted after so many sad defeats.

An Epilogue

The Seer
A ¼ Act Play.

Tiresias

"I am Tiresias, the seer of the Gods. I know what has happened, what is happening, and those events that will ever happen. In short, when it comes to knowing their business regards the past, present, and future, I'm your main man. I will tell you about those you have seen, both major and minor, in a manner which was determined by the ancient Gods.

Millicent Rothstein will live out a long life; she will become very active in theater, and remain a wonderful, beautiful, and giving person. She will never marry, for mortal men are ignorant unfeeling stumps, unable to perceive real beauty as our hero Student Patterson did. She and Student, by the way, will stay in touch and remain friends always.

Jessica Bolton will become a successful author. She will live in New York and have a rich and colorful life as a part of that city's literary set. Her twin daughters — exotic beauties — will become super models and will be seen all over the world on the covers of various publications. The three will not stay in touch with Student, but always remember him fondly, and he, them.

Mr. and Mrs. Patterson never go to

Florida, but live long and happy lives in Iowa. Mr. Patterson raises chickens — fine chickens — up to the very end, which is peaceful and graced with kindness. Beverly Patterson then moves into town, and becomes an active and content grandmother and lives a long, long time. Lila Patterson, Student's aunt, goes on shocking people for many years, and passes peacefully while Walking For Equality.

Simon Conners will die alone, yet at his funeral there will be many friends who shared his vision of the world, including Milly, of course. Davy Boy fools everyone by taking the pledge and becoming a tuba player for the Salvation Army Regional Band; however, he retains his view of capitalism always.

And Student and Debbie? They do spend a reconstructive summer together, then go to Seattle as a family. Before their departure, there is an ugly scene between Student and his father-in-law when Student severely takes the man to task for his thoughtless treatment of his family. The elderly lion attempts to strangle Student to death on the hood of his Dodge Dart but is stopped by good Samaritans. The trauma causes the elder to have a mild stroke from which he fully recovers.

But, everyone gets by this minor glitch.

Student and Debbie lived on happily, but seers, especially I, don't want to reveal too much. Why spoil things?

So you have seen what you have seen, and

never let it be said that the great Tiresias was inaccurate in what the unknowable Fates have long ordained."

— the end —

Irving Warner was born in Modesto, California in 1941 and graduated from San Francisco's Balboa High School. He soon became involved in tournament chess, playing in the first Arthur Stamer Invitational Tournament at the Mechanics Institute.

He moved to Alaska in 1964 where he lived until 1996. During that time, he initially worked in fisheries research, with a brief tenure in sea bird studies. He received a degree in Biology and English from the University of Alaska, Fairbanks in 1972. Switching careers at the age of 40, he received an M.A. in interdisciplinary studies from the University of Maine, Orono, in 1983. Warner began teaching at Kodiak College and the University of Alaska until he took early retirement and began full time writing.

Since then he has lived in Washington State and in Hawaii, and presently resides in Port Angeles, Washington.

www.ingramcontent.com/pod-product-compliance
Lightning Source LLC
Chambersburg PA
CBHW022012010726
47494CB00003B/1003